THE INDIA LIST

Monsoon

VIMALA DEVI

Translated by Paul Melo e Castro

LONDON NEW YORK CALCUTTA

SERIES EDITOR

Arunava Sinha

Seagull Books, 2019

First published in Portuguese as *Monção* by Vimala Devi, 1963

First published in English by Seagull Books, 2019

ISBN 978 0 8574 2 695 6

British Library Cataloguing-in-Publication Data

A catalogue record for this book is available from
the British Library

Typeset by Seagull Books, Calcutta, India

Printed and bound by WordsWorth India, New Delhi, India

Contents

After the Monsoon, a Rainbow: Reading Vimala Devi's Monção *from Contemporary Goa*

JASON KEITH FERNANDES

Monsoon, the new translation of Vimala Devi's *Monção* (1963), offers contemporary readers a rare peek into Goa as it appeared to a certain progressive Catholic elite on the eve of the Indian annexation of the territory from Portugal. A better understanding of this group allows us to gauge how much the political terrain has shifted, in Goa and the wider subcontinent, and to assess the political positions that made sense to progressive Catholics in this period.

The Trap of Language

'Nattak' offers the first echo of the present, when the protagonist laments 'the trap of language' or how ignorance of Portuguese or English frustrates social mobility. By 1961, Portuguese was no longer a foreign language. It had been integrated into local hierarchies, becoming a tool with which native elites distinguished themselves from those lower in the social order. Within the village-based quasi-feudal social system of Goa, Portuguese was, and remains, an intense marker of class. English, as Tukaram identifies, was the real means of progress, as represented by Naraina's sons, successful graduates from the University of Bombay. Their situation contrasts with that of Pedru in 'Hope'. Despite education in Portuguese, Pedru's chances remain dependent on the connections of his 'bhatcars' or landlords. English, however, allowed Goans access to the more dynamic world of the British Empire and the anonymity of its urban centres.

Language is still a central issue in Goa, where it is used by local elites to hobble marginalized Goans. We can see this in the Medium of Instruction (MoI) debates revolving around state support to schools where Hindu nationalists demand that only Konkani or Marathi be supported, ostensibly to encourage Goans to educate their children in those tongues. While proponents of vernacular-language instruction argued that education in English 'de-nationalized' students who should instead be educated in 'local' languages in order to inculcate nationalist virtues, in truth the mobilization against English is also undertaken for two other reasons: to halt the flight of the Hindu Bahujan from Marathi-language schools, and to harass English-medium, especially Catholic-run, institutions which marginalized groups used to escape the feudal system so vividly illustrated in *Monsoon*. The issue has emerged once again in recent years, when marginalized groups demanded state aid for instruction in English, arguing that Hindu nationalist leaders educated their own children in that language. Just like Tukaram, contemporary Bahujan have identified English as the language of escape.

The Rise and Fall of the Progressive Goan Catholic

If one thing has changed in Goa since 1961, it is the tenability of Devi's progressive Catholic position. Paul Melo e Castro observes that Devi 'portrays a Goa that veers sharply from colonial discourse' and shakes off the 'excesses of colonial ideology'.[1] First, by adopting the Indian nationalist compliant *nom de plume* Vimala Devi (though her baptismal name is Teresa da Piedade de Baptista Almeida). Second, by opening and closing *Monsoon* with Hindu protagonists, thereby challenging the rhetoric of the Estado Novo, the authoritarian Portuguese regime headed by prime minister António de Oliveira Salazar which articulated, in the face of Indian belligerence, that Goa was dominantly Catholic and unproblematically European. Given that *Monsoon* was published in Lisbon while the Estado Novo still challenged the Indian occupation of Goa, these were courageous moves on Devi's part.

Her bravura typified the progressive Goan Catholic elite critique of the colonial arrangement of power. While their claims may not have the same emotive oppositionality as British Indian demands for independence, they were no less significant. Unlike British Indians who were merely colonial subjects, all Goans were citizens of Portugal. Nevertheless, these Goan progressives demanded greater autonomy from the metropole by stressing their difference, and often superiority, to their metropolitan counterparts.

Monsoon should be seen within the context of these demands for a rearrangement of power. As Devi's stories make obvious, this elite did not fight merely for its own survival but also on behalf of diverse elements in Goa, whether Hindu or Catholic marginalized castes, or indeed the Hindu upper castes themselves.

Monsoon showcases the diversity of Goa, presenting not just Catholics and Hindus but diverse caste and class groups within these two often monolithically conceived groups. And this diversity is not limited to 'native' groups, but also includes metropolitan Portuguese and the mixed-race 'descendentes' who, though integral parts of the Goan polity, are today represented as foreign.

If on the one hand Devi represents groups invisible today, on the other *Monsoon* is marked by the occlusion of Goan Muslims. There is no reference to Muslim communities at all. This omission is notable, especially since contemporary writers like Epitácio Pais, Orlando da Costa, and Maria Elsa da Rocha all include Muslim characters in their work. Could British Indian nationalism, which stigmatized Muslim communities in India, have cast its long shadow over Devi?

If the Indian nationalism contributed to an occlusion of Muslim communities in Goa, then progressive Catholic *noblesse oblige* that sought to highlight social diversity ensured that the liberal Catholic intelligentsia scripted itself out of history, eventually marginalizing all Catholics in Goa by celebrating the Hindu subject as the ideal citizen of the territory and failing to reckon with the entrenched casteism of dominant Hindu groups. Seeing themselves as denationalized and lacking a 'genuine' Indian identity or a vibrant culture, the Catholic elite sought to unlearn European ways imbibed over centuries and inculcate 'Indian-ness' instead, taking their cue from elite Hindus, in particular, the Saraswat Brahmins, the dominant Hindu caste in Goa.

While the Catholic elite's cultural sterility is moot, the creativity of Bahujan Catholics, especially outside Goa, is incontestable, as is particularly evident in the vibrant production in literature, theatre (tiatr), film and music in 1950s Bombay. With their first letters and a rudimentary musical education, working-class Goans found employment in the British Empire and beyond. It is significant, therefore, that *Monsoon* does not reflect their agency but, rather, portrays them as suffering victims, whether it be the fisherfolk in 'Job's Children', the petitioning tenant in 'Hope' or the cowed mundcar Gustin in 'Tiatr'. Although Devi represents shifts in the *ancient régime* effected by the actions of these groups, represented by young men returning from the big cities with money and confidence—objects of desire for women such as Carminha in 'Job's Children' and sources of anxious anger to bhatcars such as Dias in 'Tiatr'—*Monsoon* nevertheless lacks a dynamic Catholic Bahujan protagonist.

In this light, the fact that *Monsoon* begins and ends with Hindu protagonists and that its mostly submissive female Hindu characters are presented as exemplary figures of their sex seems to be no coincidence and is perhaps a reflection of how Orientalism configured political thought and practice in the subcontinent during the author's formative years. Frustrated by the British failure to recognize them as imperial citizens, British Indian elites began a demand for independence predicated on a narrow nativism, constructing an image of Indian culture with ideas of the bucolic, spiritual East. The authentic citizen subject that resulted was an upper-caste Hindu male, the son of Mother India, a national mother defined by virtues ascribed to upper-caste north Indian women. It now became the pious obligation of the nationalist to protect the Indian nation and the rhetorically deified woman from foreign gaze and desire—as echoed in Dr Sirvoicar's 'protection' of his daughter Padmini from the metropolitan João Fidalgo—and to embody this narrowly defined Indian-ness in clothing and behavioural stereotypes. Additionally, Devi's Hindu characters are represented as both repositories of ancient knowledge—as evidenced by Dr Sirvoicar's rather classical and scriptural explanation of his daughter Padmini's name—*and* the harbingers of change. In 'The Cure', it is Caxinata who proposes a love above caste and creed. Furthermore, in 'Job's Children', it is the Hindu, and Brahmin, Dr Amoncar who represents not only modern science but also, in his refusal of the Christian Dona Lavínia's appeal to a common Brahmin identity, fulfils the role of ideal secular citizen.

With the Brahmanized Hindu enshrined as ideal citizen subject and harbinger of the ideal future, it was natural that Catholics be seen as faulty embodiments of Indian identity. Indeed, the pseudonym Devi can be ascribed to the power of discourses that suggested that Goan Catholics with baptismal names like hers were denationalized and hence not ideal representatives of the new India.

The term 'denationalized' entered Goan discourse in 1944 via Tristão de Bragança Cunha's pamphlet *Denationalisation of the Goans.*[2] Hailed after 1961 by the Indian state and its Goan votaries as the Father of Goan Nationalism, Cunha argued that Goan Catholics had been denationalized, or alienated, from Indian identity and race pride through Portuguese institutions like the education system, the press and the Church. Drawing from Romanticism, Cunha claimed that merely imitating the West could not produce a vibrant culture. Indeed, this argument had already been made in Francisco João da Costa's novel *Jacob e Dulce* (1898), in which the author mercilessly lampoons the manners of the Catholic gentry.[3]

Devi herself follows in Costa's satiric footsteps in her descriptions of the affected Fonseca sisters in 'The House Husband'. However, while Costa emulated Portuguese realist Eça da Queiroz's mockery of the Portuguese elite's attempts to mimic the French and the English, both Cunha and Devi were writing in a different environment—where meaning was made in the shadow of nationalist politics in British India, where dominant castes, especially the upper caste elite of the Gangetic plains and Bengal, were defining the emerging terrain of Indian identity.

Another thread in *Monsoon* that ties in with denationalization is the idea of Portuguese alienating learners from their community if they belonged to a social echelon that was not traditionally Portuguese-speaking. This sentiment is expressed in 'Nattak' where Tukaram reflects that studies in Portuguese would have created a barrier 'between him and his family, between him and his community'; and again in 'Returning', when Chandracanta, freshly back from Portugal, voices his dissatisfaction with life in the land of his ancestors. Reading this collection today, several factors suggest that Devi may have intended this final story as a pointed lesson for Catholic Goans.

The ultimate effect of the orientalism and the adoption of British-Indian nationalist notions of Indian-ness has been to hamper the ability of the Goan Catholic to represent Goan-ness and to foster a vicious Hindu nationalism that now dominates not only Indian but also Goan popular discourse.

Options for a Sociopolitical Order

But the ceding of legitimacy to a narrowly defined Indianness has done more than create a space for a brutal Hindu nationalism. The critique of European or Western manners created a space for the assertion of indigenous etiquette and morality. It was perhaps Orientalist fantasy, or nationalist self-assuredness, that masked the fact that public civility has no part in Brahmanical codes. Our contemporary vantage point shows quite clearly that what replaced a disparaged European etiquette was an assertion of caste values; in other words, the exercise of brute power. The contrast between these two forms of public behaviour can be illustrated by the fracas caused by Franjoão's attempt to eat a mango without cutlery in 'The House Husband'. The story limits itself to mocking the Catholic elite obsession with 'keep[ing] up our good name' and deliberately trivializes the issue. But the key to what was in fact at stake in the manner in which mangoes can be eaten is revealed early in the description of Franjoão's behaviour. After peeling the skin of the fruit, Franjoão smears 'his face with juice in the process' of eating it. Perhaps the sisters' objection to their brother-in-law's comportment was based on the belief that pleasure must be subjugated to form. In other words, that social behavior only emerges once personal desire is disciplined by a consideration of others.

Today dismissed as 'Portuguese leftovers', perhaps this etiquette could renew meaningful sociopolitical interactions and salvage the public sphere. My argument here is not about the superiority of the European over the South Asian, which is a mistake elements of the Goan elite may have made, a great proportion of whom were fiercely protective of their caste prerogatives and, in all likelihood, not particularly civil to those they saw as 'beneath' them. Though the building of a civil society *cannot* be limited to polite behaviour, etiquette *is* critical to forming a public platform. It is disastrous that European formats previously internalized by Goans have been discarded without the adoption of other forms discharging a similar function.

Bereft of a culture that stresses dignity and regard for others, that is, keeping up a good name through proper and ethical behaviour, the Goan polity is today marked by the dominance of persons not unlike the figure of Carlos Siqueira in 'The Future and the Past'. Adrift from family and community, Siqueira's acquisitiveness precludes the satisfaction of his most basic emotional needs. Likewise, in Goa today, marked by the excesses of the mining industry as well as the sale of Goan land to speculators catering to status consumption by British Indians, what matters is the unrestrained accumulation of capital and political power and, subsequently, its naked exhibition. The politics of the Goan Catholics who saw themselves as progressives may have inadvertently opened Goa to Hindu nationalism, neoliberalism and a collapse of the incipient public sphere.

Yet Devi's stories did more than augur the Hindu nationalism that marks our times. Built on a commitment to an egalitarian social order, the recognition of local diversity and an emphasis on the unconscionable inequalities that marked her world, they also held the potential to chart a different course for politics in Goa.

The human misery engendered by the bhatcar system is a significant thread running through Devi's stories. As in 'The House Husband', landlords lived in a comfort whose source was the labour of starving tenants. We see various orders of misery, ranging from the desperate poverty of the fisherman Bostião ('Job's Children') and the mundcars Mogrém and Vitol ('The Arms of Venus') to the youthful frustration of Tukaram ('Nattak') and Pedru ('Hope') to the gendered crushing of individual dignity in the figures of Franjoão ('The House Husband') and Angélica ('Uncertainty') to Padmini in her eponymous narrative and Dhruva in the two stories in which she features. Indeed, Devi's underlying message is that the system dehumanized everyone, albeit to different extents. While the Curumbins of Orlim are reduced to a life in which toil and paddy are 'the central reasons for their existence', both elite women *and* men are reduced to pawns in the game of petty dynastic politics.

Caste in the Goan Polity

Devi's critical gaze includes caste, perhaps the most dehumanizing institution there is. To quote Rohith Vemula, a Dalit scholar driven in 2016 to suicide by casteist and Hindu nationalist persecution, in the caste system 'the value of a man [is] reduced to his immediate identity and nearest possibility'. Devi in these stories constantly stresses the arrogance and gendered nature of caste.

'Hope' suggests that caste was not simply a matter of classifying those perceived today as local. Rather, the system also included metropolitan Portuguese and the descendentes. In the conversation between the siblings in 'Hope', the disregard of Catholic Brahmins for both the Shudras who laboured for them and the metropolitan Portuguese is on open display. Mitzi's remark that the latter are 'stupid, haven't you noticed?' provides an insight into how Europeans (and the descendentes) were dismissed by local dominant castes. However, Devi's depiction of the descendentes in 'The Supplement' is subtler. Here the protagonist Eucaristino is presented as 'so esteemed by his colleagues that he even had a few Hindu friends which was quite rare for a descendente'. This is Devi's tongue-in-cheek way of indirectly alluding to their reputation as bigots and racists. Some in contemporary Goa still recount stories of descendentes seeking to humiliate the groups identified as natives, especially Hindus. But this narrative ignores the manner in which the descendentes were often scorned by native dominant castes, both Hindu and Catholic.

Caste is a system that bows to power. While dominant castes engage with the powerful yet make no secret of their subsequent need for ritual purification, persons seen as lower are quite literally treated as sub-human. The descendentes experienced a slow social decline, triggered by the loss to the Marathas in 1739 of the Província do Norte (the Province of the North which contained territories in modern-day Gujarat and Maharashtra). By the twentieth century, the descendentes, who could only access positions in the administrative bureaucracy and public offices (such as the telegraph and post offices, the police and public works), now found themselves vying with the dominant Catholic and Hindu castes for the same jobs. In 'The Supplement', the characters are presented as sympathetic but clownish, reflecting the manner in which the descendentes were dismissed locally.

It was in the late nineteenth century, when Europeans looked down on non-Europeans and their casteism, that the descendentes first began the practices that Devi gently mocks in 'The Supplement', such as eating 'European' food in a 'European' manner, abjuring other culinary tastes, and claiming purer European ancestries. Caught between two worlds, neither of which accepted mixed-race groups, it made more sense for the descendentes to claim European identities; especially in the early years of the Estado Novo, when through the Acto Colonial of 1930 the regime sought to mimic dominant models of colonialism and institute a hierarchical difference between whites and other groups.

There is a thought-provoking parallel, however, between the dismissal of the descendentes and that of Goan Catholics today by some segments of the Indian and even Goan population. In a polity marked by dominant-caste Hindu privilege and the disparagement of racial and cultural admixture, the fate of the descendentes has to an extent presaged that of native Catholics. It is as if Goan politics were a game of musical chairs—when the music stops, those least approximating savarna Hinduism are ousted.

I would like to believe that Devi wove a possible solution to such attitudes into one of her stories. While a plausible reading of the 'The Cure' decodes a reference to abortion, I prefer to think that, like Dr B. R. Ambedkar in *The Annihilation of Caste* (1936), Devi is suggesting that the route out of the caste system is love across caste, creed and class. Here the title would refer not to the termination of pregnancy but the ability to love the eventual child regardless of dehumanizing classifications. Love is the cure. If Caxinata here is the improbable prophet of change, other unlikely prophets emerge at other points, such as the metropolitan João Fidalgo who, unbound by caste, not only seeks merely to love beyond caste but also helps a native man he barely knows (Padmini's brother in Lisbon). There is also the genuine respect that Lieutenant Gama seems to have for local culture. Compared with Roberto and his sister's dismissal of the metropolitans in 'Hope', these men emerge as relatively humane, rising above the casteism and patriarchy of the locals. In any case, these two figures evade standard representations of the arrogant white man that pro-Indian nationalist rhetoric promotes.

Catholic 'Conscience' as a Saving Grace

In two stories, Devi shows the salving role that Catholicism could play in stirring the conscience of those who would otherwise mistreat others. In 'The Arms of Venus', the bhatcar's 'conscience ordered mercy for the mundcars but Dias was unwilling to give in.' Those familiar with Catholic social teaching, as Devi would have been in the years leading up to the Vatican Council II (1962–65), know that it informs the conscience. This education of the conscience through Catholic faith is more obvious in 'Job's Children' when bhatcan Dona Lavínia's confessor impels her to relinquish a caste pride antithetical to God's word.

Though Devi unconsciously reproduced British-Indian nationalist tropes that saw Catholicism as a violation of a natural indigenous order, her work nevertheless recognized the balm of Catholicism on a polity that might otherwise have been quite merciless. Despite its bad press, especially in the wider colonial context, early modern Catholicism played an emancipatory role in Goa by substantially refashioning the established caste order, especially by removing the sting of ritual pollution that adheres to the body in the Brahmanical order. Stripped of pollution, caste could become just another form of social hierarchy, like those in many other parts of the world, Europe included.

One gets a glimmer of this class dimension of Catholic caste in 'The House Husband' when the Brahmin spinsters suggest that they are willing to entertain the idea of a Chardó match because Joaquim Menezes comes from 'a *good* Chardó family. Ancient and noble' (emphasis added). Capital provided the motivation to, at least momentarily, ignore caste. Devi's description of the entire business of marriage leaves us in no doubt about the pragmatism involved in matrimonial transactions.

The introduction of Catholicism, and the linking of local elites to Europe, ensured that caste could be reinterpreted through a European lens. Thus, being Chardó or Brahmin was interpreted, especially among elite members of these castes, as being noble, an interpretation made possible by a strategy in use from at least the seventeenth to the twentieth century. As mentioned previously, caste in Goa was located not in Brahmanical purity but in noble ancestry. Such was the efficacy of this strategy that even in contemporary Portugal, for those to whom such things matter, Brahmins or Chardós are still viewed as nobles.

This reinterpretation was not merely for the Portuguese but also internalized by dominant-caste Catholics, as evidenced in Devi's stories. In 'Decline', 'the ancient Brahmin traditions so hallowed in our family' have nothing to do with what is popularly associated with Brahmins. They speak of commanding the service and respect of servants and tenants, of delicate and discrete social etiquette, of *noblesse oblige*. To be Brahmin was to embody noble behaviour. This way of being a Catholic Brahmin needed no reference to Hindu Brahmanism, guided as it was by a different ideology. Of course, this ideal stands in contrast to the pathetic cry of Dona Lavínia to Dr Amoncar: 'Like you, I too am a Brahmin.' Such a cross-religious reference would have been possible only once Orientalism and British-Indian nationalism had defined the Hindu Brahmin as the pinnacle of the South Asian social order.

Monsoon and Goa after the Portuguese

The overall impression caused by *Monsoon* is of a polity teetering blindly on the brink of upheaval. No one is happy with their lot. Tenants want more, and are either migrating as in 'Nattak', acquiring new skills as in 'Hope' or challenging the rei(g)n of the landlords as in 'Tiatr'. Indeed, in this story, Bhatcar Dias even predicts that 'it wouldn't be long before mundcars and bhatcars were all lumped together'. Devi must have perceived that the bhatcar system was on its last legs. In 'Decline', the death of the Africanista son begins the downward spiral of the family. While the grandmother's demise is presented as the moment of collapse, the question we should ask is: If the estate sufficed to keep the family, why would the son migrate? Numerous stories—including 'The House Husband' and 'The Future and the Past'—indicate that such estates required external funds for their maintenance. It fell upon sons to leave in search of funds in order to return homes to their former, or imagined, grandeur.

In this context, knowing that a tidal wave of revolt was coming, one wonders how the situation would have played out had India not annexed Goa. The immediate post-1961 period was dominated by the Maharashtrawadi Gomantak

Party (MGP), Goa's first ruling political party and one which espoused the cause of the tenants. These years were in many ways a liberation for the Bahujan, with the destruction of the bhatcar system, the expansion of the welfare state and an empowerment of the tenant, at least in the Old Conquests.[4] Yet critics claim this agenda was not carried out wholeheartedly: the landlords in the New Conquests retained their properties and a bias towards Brahmanical Hinduism, which shifted the political field towards Hindu nationalism, was institutionalized. The MGP mobilized the Hindu Bahujan though right-wing appeals, employing strategies that would be repeated during the language agitations of the 1980s that date to the early twentieth century, embodied by the Nattak in Devi's first story. Kaustubh Naik suggests that plays—which focused on Puranic myths and the Maratha ruler Shivaji—acted as a catalyst in an environment that forged discrete caste groups into a Hindu public.[5] Given that the MGP espoused a cause that united tenants, Hindus and Marathi, and used a rhetoric that lumped Catholics, Brahmins and landlords together, the de facto Hindu nationalism and lack of alternative Catholic voices from the landed castes and classes, playing out the script contained in Devi's stories where the bhatcars are unable to acclimate themselves to a rapidly advancing new order, contributed to the poisoning of the Goan polity and whose seeds—represented in the elements, actions and characters of Devi's stories—were already present in *Monsoon*.

* * *

Given the breadth of her critique, and the possibilities for political action it suggested, it is tragic that *Monsoon* was published in a language smothered after Goa's annexation and a translation not made widely available in English and Konkani previously. It is also tragic that authors such as Devi who articulated a cogent critique of their own class were relegated to oblivion after 1961. This is partly due to the fear generated by the Indian state among Portuguese speakers and the suppression of the language in Indian Goa. Fortunately, with translations like *Monsoon*, the veil that was dropped after 1961 is beginning to lift.

Notes

1 Paul Melo e Castro, 'How the Other Half Lives: Representing the Subaltern in the Lusophone Goan Short Story', Modern Languages Association Convention (Los Angeles, 6–9 January 2011).

2 T. B. Cunha, 'The Denationalization of Goans' in *Goa's Freedom Struggle: Selected Writings of T. B. Cunha* (Bombay: Dr. T. B. Cunha Memorial Committee, 1961), pp. 55–98.

3 Gip (Francisco João da Costa), *Jacob & Dulce: Sketches from Indo-Portugese Life* (Alvaro Noronha da Costa trans.) (New Delhi: Sahitya Akademi, 1896).

4 Goa has traditionally been divided into the Velhas Conquistas (Old Conquests) and the Novas Conquistas (New Conquests). Comprising the concelhos or talukas of Ilhas (today known as Tiswadi), Bardez, Salcete and Mormugão and containing the major towns of Panjim, Mapuça, Margão and the port city of Vasco da Gama, the Old Conquests were under Portuguese control from the 1500s until the early twentieth century and were populated almost entirely by Catholics. They form the core of the territory of Goa. Conquered in the seventeenth century, and comprising a buffer zone, as it were, the New Conquests include the concelhos of Pernem, Bicholim, Sanquelim, Satari, Ponda, Sanguem, Quepem and Canacona and have always been inhabited predominantly by non-Catholics (including Muslims and castes that today identify as Hindu).

5 Kaustubh Naik, 'Jhalach Pahije: Arguing for Goa's merger with Maharashtra', 17th International Conference on Maharashtra: Language and Power, University of Chicago Centre (New Delhi, 5–7 January 2017).

A Note on the Translation

Portuguese-era versions of proper names have been retained as relics of the historical time these stories depict and the language in which they were originally written. Places such as Pangim, Mapuçá, Margão and Badém thus keep their Portuguese orthography and diacritics and Hindu names retain their Portuguese transliteration (so, Naraina as opposed to Narayana; Sirvoidcar not Shirwaikar, etc.). Perhaps the gap between these unfamiliar spellings and today's usage signals that between Goa now and the bygone Goa represented in *Monsoon*.

The fictional village of Orlim, in which many of these stories are set, is a thinly disguised version of the author's natal Britona. It is not to be confused with the real Orlim, which lies not on the placid banks of the Mandovi in Bardez but on the shores of the Indian Ocean in Salcete.

The tree's shadow stretches away at sundown
Without ever splitting from it

Kalidasa

She made her way with difficulty through the crowd outside the temple. In the midst of the throng, on a makeshift stage out in the open air, a *rasa* of love was being performed. But not everybody could watch the show; only those sitting closest, on the side benches, sprawling at the front, on mats, or standing up and forming an outer circle. Half the audience was happy just to hear the actors. Many others still, who could neither see nor hear them, ate the spicy snacks and slurped the aromatic tea hawked by street vendors. A heavy aroma of chondor-vatt, bidis, spices and the scent of flowers tucked decoratively into women's hair drifted up from the multitude.

People were there from all the villages nearby, drawn in by the renown of this nattak. As she had been, though she came from afar, from another district, not wanting to miss her chance to see Jayadeva's famed drama. Not so much for the plot, which she knew, but for one of the actors, for Tukaram, whose fame had spread throughout the surrounding villages.

She made her way through the crowd, stumbling over the outstretched legs until she could see the stage. There Radha sang of the pain caused by her beloved Krishna's long absence. Just then the *raibari*, her confidante, announced:

In these intoxicating days
That make separation so cruel to lovers
The young Hari grows giddy and dances
with a group of young ladies.

The melody spooled out in a languid rhythm that thrilled those who heard it. Durga remained where she stood, eyes open, alert, imagining fabulous scenes from days long past, when the gods came down to earth and walked among men, before the advancing Aryan invaders usurped the Dravidians in their own land . . .

When the melody ceased, the crowd applauded, yelling and laughing and clapping their hands. Durga laughed happily along too, until she felt a sudden thirst. She had walked a long way to attend the nattak. Besides, there in the crush, though out in the open, it was unbearably hot. Wanting to get herself a soft drink, she began to thread her way through the swarm. Next to the stage, however, the mass of spectators had clumped together in an attempt to fit into the same space. 'How tiresome!' she thought. But her thirst spurred her on, and forward she burrowed. Unexpectedly, she found herself right up at the front. She had been diverted by the crowd.

She shook her head in frustration. She needed to make her way over to the other side, to where the street vendors were. And now there was only one route to get there: across the stage. Shilly-shallying, not daring to walk over with so many people watching, she gazed on in vexation. Suddenly she clicked her fingers. She could go by the rear of the stage, safe from peering eyes. No one would be able to see her. Laughing with satisfaction, she resolutely pushed aside the drapes and darted in. An intrepid girl, there was no doubt about it. However, a few steps later, her courage vanished into thin air when she stumbled across Krishna in his lushly shining robes and blue face paint. He looked at her in surprise.

'A young actress, or a goddess descended from heaven?' he asked, barring her path.

Without quite realizing how, Durga felt her shyness melt away, and was shocked to hear herself say: 'Why are you painted that colour?'

The actor frowned, disconcerted. It was obvious he had not expected her to answer back. In any other circumstance he would have ordered the intruder to leave, but there was something in the girl's demeanour that compelled a response:

'I'll explain on condition that you go away, OK? Backstage is only for actors . . . Look: I'm Krishna, the Dravidian god, so I have to be dark-coloured. Now you go back to your place, eh? Go back to your place, what're you waiting for?'

'I wanted a soda . . . ' Durga stammered awkwardly.

He towered over her and laughed, displaying pearly white teeth.

'A soda. Deva! Imagine that! But it's impossible just now. Can't you see the third act is about to begin?' Almost without realizing it, he stroked her long, black plait. He blinked, then gazed at her steadily. For a moment he was silent, then 'Wait!' he blurted, 'Stay here quietly, behind the curtain, until this scene has finished . . . then we can go and find something to drink!'

'But I want to see Tukaram,' Durga whispered.

'Well, then, you already have. Because I'm Tukaram!' Krishna exclaimed and he strode off to make his entrance.

Durga was left alone and confused. She squatted down on her heels, between the edge of the stage and the set, in silence. Her head spun. 'Could that really be him?' Mentally she made a comparison with the photograph on the flyer handed out in the villages. She had kept one for herself and . . . in truth, if you looked closely . . . 'If Aai knew that I . . . ,' she thought. But the sudden memory of her mother brought sadness in its wake. She didn't know exactly what was going on, some trouble with her and her mother that Durga couldn't understand. Nobody in their neighbourhood spoke to them. And so, for no apparent reason, Durga found herself beset by loneliness. One day, as her mother combed out her long hair and anointed it with coconut oil, she enquired timidly: 'Aai, why don't you ever speak about Dadda? Mogrém asked me yesterday who my father was . . . '

'Let her ask,' her mother retorted. 'I'll break her face if she keeps sticking her nose into my life.' She glared at her daughter for a moment. 'Hum, dadda!' she snorted, then spat out of the window in disgust.

That gesture on her mother's part hurt for all it might suggest, were she to allow it. Were she to allow it . . . but Durga didn't want to think, at heart she didn't want to know, for she had a hidden fear of what she might discover. Aai spent so much time away from home, and left her so alone . . .

'Aai, don't go out today,' she'd said.

Her mother looked back in surprise.

'I have to, Durga! I have to! Is there something you want?'

No, Durga thought. She wanted for nothing. She had beautiful dresses, jewellery, good food. But she was always so alone . . . . And she had no father. She had no dadda.

The painful memory of her mother, of her solitude, of all her unhappy thoughts evaporated when the audience began to applaud the final scene.

Although you are far away
And given over to wild reverie of other beauties,
My spirit is laden with your image
and with your touch . . .

She looked up. Krishna was returning from his reverie to the arms of the inconsolable Radha whom he'd taken as his divine wife. The final song, of mankind and mystical love, had poured forth from Tukaram's lips until the curtain fell. From her hiding place Durga saw the blue-coloured god thank the audience for their applause and then cross the stage in her direction. Her heart pounded with excitement. Again, she heard Radha's nostalgic song:

'Although you are far from me . . . My spirit is laden with your image . . .' and then *'And with your touch . . .'* a line that left Durga oddly flustered. But the blue-coloured god had passed her by. He had forgotten all about his admirer.

'Tukaram!' she called, plucking up her courage.

He stopped short and peered around. Seeing Durga in the same spot he had left her, he laughed out loud.

'Are you still here? Do you still want that drink? Just let me take off this costume and wash my face, so that I'm myself again, OK?'

'My house is very far from here,' Durga replied a little awkwardly, 'I must leave while people are going in my direction.'

'All the better,' Tukaram exclaimed cheerfully. 'Let them go their own sweet way. I'll take you home afterwards, on my bike.'

With that, he disappeared backstage. When he returned, moments later, he was chewing betel and clad in white trousers and an untucked shirt. He was a handsome figure, fair-skinned, and possessed of poise and self-confidence. Inwardly, he relished having made such an impression on an admirer, now glancing up at him furtively. Placing his hand on her long plait, he guided her towards a small eating house.

'I'm absolutely starving,' he announced as soon as they were seated. 'I'll have some xacuti. Do you want some too?'

She couldn't contain herself. She was like a timid little animal, fearful of facing the unknown but also audacious, like the small wild creatures. For the first time she was with a man, and a great actor, one who had even played the role of Krishna. This filled her with such excitement she could barely follow what he was saying.

'I'd like to see you in a sari, with nothing underneath . . .'

'Aai has promised to buy me one,' she answered innocently. 'She says I'm old enough to wear a sari now.'

Her words made him pause. How old was she? She looked like an adult.

'Aai says I was five when Babu the grocer died. But everyone thinks I look older.'

Tukaram didn't answer. Babu had died eleven years ago. He knew this better than anyone—for he was Babu's son. It had been eleven years since his father died. That meant she must be sixteen, no more than a child. He regretted having misjudged her. In any case, he had begun to think fondly of the girl. Her childlike reactions and the naivety with which she had approached him during the nattak inspired a great tenderness within him.

'Here come our xacutis. What would you like to drink?'

'Soda!'

'A soda and some hot tea!'

Just the an old white-haired man got up hurriedly from a nearby table and shuffled over with a smile on his face.

'What joy!' he exclaimed, stretching out his arms. 'Aren't you Tukaram, son of my friend Babu Candolcar?'

Tukaram looked up and frowned in surprise.

'Yes, I am,' he said. 'And you are . . . let me see if I remember . . . ah! You must be . . . . Wait! You're Naraina! But hadn't you gone to Bombay? Just look, old Naraina, here with me. Who would have said? How's tricks with Dinanata? But, first, please do take a seat, please.'

'I see that you recognize me,' said Naraina, casting a sidelong glance at Durga. 'Dinanata is in Delhi and will make his film debut any day now. What about you? What are you waiting for? When I saw you walk in, I decided to come over and congratulate you on your fine performance in the nattak, and I swear: you've got talent. You shouldn't fritter it away in Goa. There is no scope for artists here . . . ' Twisting in his chair, he called the waiter over.

'If you're calling him for me, I thank you,' Tukaram murmured 'but I don't want anything else.' He felt embarrassed at not knowing his young companion's name. He faltered for a moment, then said: 'But I don't know if my cousin would like . . . '

'Ah, your cousin? How do you do?' said the old man gently, giving a little wave. 'I'll order you some tea.'

Durga returned his greeting with a smile, declining his offer with a shake of her head.

'Just the one tea,' Naraina said, before turning to the boy and continuing: 'Get yourself off to Bombay, Tukaram. Study the dramatic arts—don't waste your artistic gifts . . . . An artist is like a plant that needs watering every day! Here in Goa sprout seeds that out there can grow into great talents . . . the dung beetle never stays in the dung.

Sometimes such seeds shrivel up for lack of resources, or social support, or because they belong to a humble caste, but they always have a chance to succeed. I think so often of your father! So many times I'd advised him to leave: "Get out of here, Babu, you weren't made to sell coconuts and jaggery." But what . . . '

There was no room for doubt in Tukaram's mind. Naraina must have been his father's best friend. But did he know the whole truth: that his father had squandered his meagre savings on a temple dancer whom he then left out of remorse for having driven his wife to an early grave? Did he know that Babu had died an alcoholic, leaving his children crippled with debt? Did he not know that? He stared at Naraina, trying to divine his innermost thoughts, but the old man's eyes told him nothing. Tukaram preferred to hold his peace. Besides, Durga was there . . . The girl had been so desperate to meet the great Tukaram!

Noting the silence of the two youngsters, Naraina apologized for intruding. He had come over with the best of intentions but it had perhaps been wrong to butt in. He thought back over his words but could find nothing that might have caused offence. Perhaps it was his point of view that had been unwelcome. Regretful for having acted on an impulse, he rose to leave.

'I wish to thank you in my father's name!' Tukaram said, standing up in turn. 'He too was a great idealist. When I was a boy, he made me go to school . . . all he lacked was the courage to do something with his life.'

Old Naraina sat down once more. It pained him to leave without imparting some advice to this young man, who was so full of talent but who would surely end up like his father. It pained him; he felt duty-bound to speak up while there was still time. Looking Tukaram in the eye, he said: 'Tukaram, you know that I was a great friend of your father's. Perhaps his best. We talked about our dreams so many times. We wanted to make something of our lives. I was crushed by the idea of running a tavern—my father's only legacy. What was more, if I sacrificed my future I would also destroy my children's. What could I do? Like Babu, I spoke no Portuguese! So I plucked up courage and left with my family for Bombay. I suffered moments of adversity, always with one eye on my sons' education. But I worked hard and my toil was rewarded: my youngest qualified as an architect and Dinanata has gone into acting . . . Babu preferred to stay here, and you know the result . . .'

To inspire the son of his great friend was a sacred duty for old Naraina. But he could never have guessed how far his advice had transported Tukaram whose inner gaze had fixed on a goal so distant as to be unreachable! Always the same problem, the problem of language! he thought. At home they spoke only Konkani; in the village no one knew Portuguese; and, as a child, before he went to Portuguese primary school, he'd learnt Marathi. What else could he do in Goa but follow in his father's profession and, in his spare time, perform in amateur nattkan?

'If you ever need me,' Naraina added, placing a card on the table, 'here's my address in Bombay!'

But Tukaram was no longer listening. He was far, far away.

* * *

The way home rose before them like an outstretched sheet as the dull glare of the bike lamp rent the darkness. Even the stars above seemed loath to share their distant glitter. Tukaram pedalled mechanically, still overcome by the emotions of the evening: first his performance in the nattak, then the unexpected appearance of Durga and, finally, the encounter with his father's old friend . . . He searched for some link that might connect these three events. Nattak—he thought—is theatre made by the people for the people, the people who gather en masse, tramping for miles each day to applaud a performance by men like him who, though uneducated, had an intimate knowledge of their dramas and their joys. Naraina himself belonged to this uneducated class, yet he had managed to save his children from the trap of language! He recalled his own case, the Portuguese he'd learnt at primary school and which, in the society of his own people, he'd eventually forgotten. For things to be any different, he would've had to leave for the city to continue his studies in Portuguese. And what then? A barrier would have been created between him and his family, between him and his community. Perhaps it was for this reason that his father had preferred to leave Tukaram uneducated, as he had been himself, as his grandfather and ancestors had been before him. But what about Naraina's boys? Ah, they'd attended the village English school, later gone to the University of Bombay . . . . Why had his father not enrolled him in an English school? Mr Fernandes' classes weren't expensive. Then it would've been so simple to get a place at university or drama school . . . . But then his mother died, his father turned to drink, his savings sucked dry long ago by his mistress.

Unlike Tukaram, whose mind churned with tortuous thoughts, Durga was enjoying a new experience. Seated between the young man's strong arms on the frame of his bike, her plait streaming out behind her, she dreamt of romance that dark night. She wanted to tell him so many things, about her lonely life and her mother's absences . . . But he . . . why was he so silent? Was he still thinking about the old man's words? How unfortunate that encounter, interrupting such a happy moment, the moment when they'd almost been alone, free to talk and talk, the moment when she might have told him about all the things in her mind . . . She disagreed vehemently with the old man's advice that Tukaram should go to Bombay. In Goa he was renowned in all the villages, from Pomburpá to Betim. It would hurt so much if he were to leave, now that she could finally see him every day!

Only the keening jackals disturbed the silence of the fields. Up ahead, the light of a candle in its coconut-shell holder guided the steps of a group of people, perhaps also returning home from the nattak.

'Those people live near me. If I had walked back with them, now I'd be arriving alone. It's much better to be in your company . . .'

This last sentence was uttered with such affection that Tukaram couldn't resist planting a kiss on her hair.

'If you'd like to see the nattak again tomorrow, come and find me. I can take you on my bicycle. What do you say?'

'Yes. I'll come tomorrow and every other night just to see you perform . . .'

'That's not much of a reason, Durga. Can't you see that I'm just an uneducated actor? If it hadn't been for Naraina, I'd have gone on in my ignorance. But now I don't have the heart to go back on stage!'

Durga stiffened. A deep sense of revolt rose within her, as if somebody was about to steal her heart's desire.

'Pay no heed!' she almost shouted. 'Let the old man prattle! He might think himself a hero for having educated his children, but we have our own way of living, simple and free of care. Here, in Goa, we can be happy too!' What she really wanted to say was: they could be happy if Tukaram wanted them to be so.

'Naraina is right, Durga! He's made me realize that if I stay ignorant, those who see me and hear me will also stay ignorant. Do you understand?'

'But you're a great actor, Tukaram! Didn't you see the photograph on the flyer? I kept one for myself . . . '

'That's just advertising, Durga. If I don't study, I'll never make anything of myself. And I want to be a great actor!'

'Like Raj Kapoor? I'm such a fan!' Durga exclaimed. 'I saw him the one time Aai took me to the cinema in Mapuçá. She never took me again because it's too far.'

They had arrived in Durga's neighbourhood. There only remained a narrow stretch of track ahead, which they bumped along as Tukaram weaved his way in and around the protruding rocks. Small mud huts, with low ceilings and walls lined with palm-leaves, stood on each side of the lane. Cats leapt from rooftop to rooftop and pigs grunted in fright as the couple passed by. In the darkness, snakes roamed free. With no need for boltholes or hiding places, some even lay outstretched on the path.

Finally, they arrived. Durga jumped down and pointed out a little house, no different from the others.

'Here it is,' she said. 'Would you like to come in?'

Tukaram gave a start. Such an invitation was the last thing he'd expected, especially after the effort he'd made all the way to remain respectful. He began to suspect that perhaps her girlish manner was feigned, a trap to ensnare him.

'At this hour? What will your parents say?'

'Nothing, I've only got Aai. And she's never home. She only gets back in the morning.'

There must be something amiss. Tukaram couldn't understand it. He was perplexed. What could the explanation be? His doubts were fast becoming certainties. Under other circumstances, he'd have gone in with no hesitation. But he couldn't just leave either. One last scruple obliged him not to judge by appearances.

Durga entered and lit the lamp, filling the kitchen with light. On the hard well-swept dung floor gleamed piles of pitchers, dishes and copper plates. From his seat out on the step, Tukaram admired Durga's serene manner and contemplated her sweet expression as she made the tea. It was the first time since his mother's death that he'd felt the intimacy of a home. Here before him was a woman. In her he saw the figure of his mother, of a woman who could lift a man to heaven or cast him down into the abyss, or, sometimes, simply leave him indifferent. To which category did

Durga belong? Everything seemed to point to the first, but Tukaram was reluctant to trust this hasty judgement. There was one way to put her to the test, but he couldn't do it! At the nattak, even for a little while afterwards, she would've been at fault, for having goaded him with questions and followed him around insistently. But what stopped him now weren't really scruples or conscience . . . it was something more . . . something . . . He noticed what time it was and felt troubled: 'It's past three! You must be sleepy!' he said.

'Sleepy? I do nothing but sleep when I'm at home. And when I'm not asleep, I'm alone. You were so kind to bring me back. Otherwise I'd just be sitting here thinking sad thoughts!' She smiled, so that her words seemed less petulant.

'Your loneliness is sister to mine, Durga!' he murmured. 'Before I go, I want to let you know that it's been a long time since I had such a nice evening.' He stood up and wandered over into the next room. He looked around him, his curious gaze taking everything in.

'I'll fetch the lamp. You'll be more comfortable here,' she said, drawing him a chair. With swift movements, she began to tidy up. Leaning over, she rolled up a mat that had been left out after her afternoon nap and placed it in the corner, behind a chest of drawers. As she swung around she knocked over a vase of flowers with her hand—it fell to the floor and shattered.

'And all because of me. I'm sorry! Why did you roll up the mat when you're going to need it out to sleep on? It's my fault. I shouldn't have come!'

Durga didn't reply. As she carefully swept the floor, Tukaram's gaze alighted on a photograph atop the chest of drawers. It showed a woman whose features resembled those of Durga: expressive eyes, a well-defined mouth, hair pulled back. If you looked closely, there was only one difference between the two faces: Durga's pensive countenance was lined slightly by a precocious sorrow.

But when he examined the picture more attentively, Tukaram gave a shudder. He stood there, frozen . . . He picked it up. He brought it closer. Those deep-set, scintillating eyes, that haughty, disdainful mouth, that high forehead, that nose . . . . Tukaram shuddered again. Now he understood everything. He understood everything that Durga couldn't. The absences, the solitude in which she lived . . . that photograph explained it all. It was a face he knew. It had once been famous throughout the district. The face of Zayu the temple dancer. Zayu, whose beauty had bewitched dozens of men. Zayu, who had bewitched Babu Candolcar, who had driven him to ruin and then to drink, who had left him bound forever to this land. It was Zayu, the temple dancer! The temple dancer Zayu, for whom his father had ruined himself, for whom he'd ignored the advice and example of his friend Naraina, the temple dancer Zayu whose fault it was that he, Tukaram, was nothing more than an uneducated actor, an amateur performer of nattakan. And this girl Durga was her daughter!

Now he understood everything . . . He felt a great sadness, deep and painful. He straightened up. On the other hand, he thought, I have my redress. What the mother took away, the daughter has given back. That talk with old

Naraina had been a decisive moment in his life. He now knew the way forward. And he might not have found it had little Durga not approached him backstage. What the mother took away . . .

Tukaram stood before the photograph like a sleepwalker. Then, slowly, he began to back away towards the door.

'Farewell, Durga! Thank you, Durga! I shall never forget you, Durga,' he whispered, retreating into the dark.

Busy wrapping the shards of vase to be thrown into the river the next day, Durga didn't notice Tukaram leave. When she heard the clatter of his bicycle, she ran out, certain to find him in the hall. But the door was open, and outside there was nothing but the darkness that had swallowed Tukaram without mercy.

She stopped at the night's edge, afraid of snakes that might slither by in the dark, imperious and free. She could hear the rattle of the bicycle as it juddered over the rocks. It was Tukaram leaving. Leaving without a word, leaving her, as everyone else had, alone in the world.

She leant against the door and waited for dawn. Her fear of snakes had long disappeared, but she dreaded going back inside and returning once more to her loneliness.

The House Husband

I

One hot, heavy day, a forewarning of the coming monsoon, tia Sacramenta arrived with news. There was nothing odd in that, for if the Fonseca sisters were up to speed with the town's tittle-tattle they owed it to her. But this time the old lady's face wore an uncommonly grave expression. She came in, kissed everyone on the cheek and sat down.

'Soledade, Claudina, Teodolinda, Dejanira!' she intoned methodically by order of their ages. 'Come here, my girls. Come sit with me.'

The sisters obeyed, taken aback by such formality. The four of them owed little to beauty or youth. Soledade was forty-nine. Short and fat, with a stern, forceful countenance, she was the head of the household. Claudina, a shade over forty, was skinny, sallow and given to sighing, burping and mouthing litanies to St Anthony. Teodolinda was going to turn thirty-eight at Christmas. She was undoubtedly the most attractive, having a certain sparkle to her eyes. As for Dejanira, the youngest, chicken pox had gnawed away at her face, leaving her with horribly pitted cheeks. It was said that she had been a beauty before her illness, from which she took a degree of solace. No one could prove it, though. She had been only nine when the affliction struck.

These hopeless spinsters lived alone in an old mansion, with no one for company but two aged servants from the time of their papa. As there hadn't been any male issue, the Fonseca line was coming to an end. Painfully resigned to see it slip into oblivion, the four sisters bewailed the lack of anyone to inherit or continue the ancient traditions of their clan.

A visit from tia Sacramenta was always a welcome distraction from the monotony of their lives. Intrigued, therefore, by the old lady's behaviour, they asked curiously: 'What's happened, ti Sacramenta?'

'What do you think? Haven't you heard?'

'Haven't we heard what?' they exclaimed in unison.

'Don't you know the news?'

'What news, ti Sacramenta?'

'Franjoão's back!'

'Franjoão who, ti Sacramenta?'

'Franjoão Barreto, from Saligão. Don't you remember him, girls?'

'Oh, yes,' Claudina exclaimed. 'I remember him well. He had a bit of a thing for Soledade, didn't he? Before he went to Africa! But she wasn't interested . . . '

'Not interested, me . . . ?' her sister protested, wringing her hands in despair.

Ti Sacramenta interjected: 'Let's not worry about that now. We're all women here and we can speak our minds. You know very well that the only thing Franjoão did was to dance once with Soledade at the club. The whole town went overboard gossiping because they were no spring chickens, but that doesn't signify. Besides, he was all set to leave. Listen, have you seen Franjoão since his return?'

'Nooooo!' they shrieked in a single frantic voice.

Ti Sacramenta laid her hands flat on the table, her fingers splayed out. She paused for a moment. Then: 'Well now! Franjoão, in truth, is hardly a catch. He's put on quite a bit of weight and lost almost all his hair. What's more, as you're well aware, he never rose beyond the post of administrative assistant. As for the financial side of things, you know the position the Barretos of Saligão are in . . . '

'They're Brahmins from Saligão!'

'None better,' ti Sacramenta agreed. 'None better, but penniless . . . '

'So?' Soledade protested. 'Blood is above money.'

'Indeed! That's just what I thought when I spoke to him this morning.'

The four sisters leant forward in unblinking excitement. 'You spoke to him this morning?'

A self-satisfied smile, full of slyness, played upon Ti Sacramenta's lips.

'I did. And it so happens that he asked after you. He said: "How are those Fonseca sisters, tia Sacramenta do Rosário? I thought I'd pay them a visit one of these days.

Not today, I have to go into the village this afternoon. Some other time." And do you know what else he asked?'

'No, ti Sacramenta!' they chorused.

'He asked: "Are they still unmarried?"'

'He was making fun!' Claudina sobbed. 'Since Papa died, everyone makes fun of us . . .'

'Nonsense!' the old lady protested. 'I saw what he was after straight away. Look: you said, quite rightly, that blood is above money. Tell me: what do you lack in this house? Haan? Isn't it a ghor-zavoim, a live-in son-in-law to continue the line?'

'You mean a brother-in-law, don't you, ti Sacramenta?' Dejanira said. The blood had drained from her face. Soledade clutched her throat, left breathless by such a thrilling prospect.

'Brother-in-law, son-in-law, it's the same thing. I thought that you might take in Franjoão. He could marry Teodolinda . . .'

'But why Teodolinda?' Soledade asked suddenly in a tremulous and slightly irked voice. 'Why not Dejanira or Claudina if we're going for one of the younger sisters? I've given up on marriage myself—I have no patience for men. But I fail to see why it should be Teodolinda and not Dejanira . . .'

But ti Sacramenta didn't let her finish: 'What are you thinking, Soledade? Can't you see that Dejanira is all pockmarked? No man will touch her, whereas Teodolinda . . .'

Dejanira burst into tears and ran sobbing from the room. A worried Teodolinda jumped up and chased after her, leaving the two elder sisters behind to discuss matters with ice-cold logic.

Ti Sacramenta grimaced. 'It's a unique opportunity, I tell you. You surely don't expect anything of those pip-squeak lawyers who come sniffing about every now and then, do you? Teodolinda is already thirty-eight . . . '

'Thirty-eight, ti Sacramenta?' Claudina objected. 'I'm thirty-six and much older. You'd be closer to the mark if you said thirty-two.'

'OK, thirty-two,' the old woman sighed. 'But she doesn't exactly have her pick of suitors.'

'What do you mean?' said Soledade. 'Only two years ago Joaquim Menezes of Santa Cruz wanted her hand . . . '

'Yes, but Joaquim Menezes is from Santa Cruz. He's a Chardó . . . '

'A good Chardó family. Ancient and noble,' Claudina chipped in vigorously.

'If his being a Chardó wasn't a problem, why didn't you accept?' asked ti Sacramenta, her voice heavy with irony. 'Look, Franjoão is hardworking, of good people . . . '

'A good family, Brahmins from Saligão,' Soledade agreed, convinced.

'An how old is he now, ti Sacramenta?' Claudina asked.

The old woman grabbed the opportunity to get her own back: 'He must be around fifty. Soledade's age . . . Ti Aureliano could arrange the match for you. Shall I ask him to relay your offer?' she asked with an indulgent smile.

II

Francisco João Barreto, better known as Franjoão, had grown fat during his ten years in Africa. He wasn't obese exactly, but, being quite short and bald, he looked rounder than he was. To cap it all, he was quite dissatisfied with life—try as he might he simply couldn't get on. At every turn he was slighted, his goodwill abused, a colleague promoted ahead of him. Yet at least he'd plucked up the courage to emigrate while his brother Franxavier had stayed behind, clinging to their land, to the decrepit old house of cracked walls that the mundcars had almost totally abandoned and which hardly brought in enough for rice and curry. Franjoão's great dream, when he had left for Mozambique, had been to save up and restore the family to its former grandeur. But it had all been in vain. Ten years had passed and with no little sacrifice he had managed finally to return to Goa for a leave of absence. But in the old house of his ancestors all he found was misery, desolation and decay: his brother overwhelmed with children; his sister-in-law Belmira, frail and haggard. The few thousand rupees he had put away weren't going to stretch very far.

But Franjoão hadn't lost his famous good spirits, which had once made him the toast of club parties and picnics. At that very moment, he was resting on a mat when Coinção informed him that ti Aureliano was there. He leapt up and hurried out to greet him.

'Ti Aureliano, how are you? Come in, come in! What are you waiting out there for? Coinção, fetch ti Aureliano something to drink. What would you like?'

'Don't bother yourself, my boy. There's no need . . . '

'It's no bother at all. Bring some orchata, Coinção.'

Ti Aureliano sat ponderously down, and then looked Franjoão square in the eye: 'It makes me very happy to see you, my boy.'

'Me too, ti Aureliano. Is tia Carmina well? I must pay her a visit one of these days.'

'You're always welcome, as you know. It's always a pleasure to see you. How about yourself? How's tricks? Are you married?'

'Me?' Franjoão laughed. 'I don't give marriage any thought. Franxavier has fulfilled our obligation to the family line. Anyway, I'm old . . . Who'd want me?' he asked, suspicion creeping into his voice.

'Come now,' ti Aureliano exclaimed. 'I bet there'd be no lack of interested parties . . . You're selling yourself short, Franjoão. What better match could they want . . . ?'

He gave a little scoff of protest: 'Chi! There's nobody interested in me, ti Aureliano. Nobody at all . . . '

'Well, I know someone who's more than interested!'

Franjoão, who'd smelt a rat all along, was immediately on his guard. If ti Aureliano bore a proposal, he'd have to box clever. He was of no age to marry in haste. It had to be a lavish offer—a good family, a good dowry that would allow him to kickstart his life. He had to play it smart and haggle well, to wring out every last advantage, so he ventured only a tentative, 'Really?'

The old man reached up and grasped the orchata that Coinção was holding out. He took a sip, slowly, and waited for the maid to leave. Then he continued: 'Oh yes, Franjoão my friend! A rich girl from a good family. No finer Brahmins. If you are in agreement . . . '

Franjoão gave nothing away: 'Really?'

'It's up to you. They're very respectable people, mind. Don't you see who I mean?'

'No.'

'Can't you guess?'

'How could I?'

'The Fonsecas of Margão.'

'Chii, ti Aureliano! What sort of half-baked proposal is this? They look like scarecrows! And they're too old. Soledade must be almost fifty now. Not to mention there's more than one sister entitled to the inheritance.'

The old man shook his head. 'You can rest assured on that score. They want a ghor-zavoim. Of the four it's Teodolinda who'll marry. She's not a bad looker, you know. They want to establish the husband. He'll be in a comfortable position, believe you me.'

'But what if they change their minds? The others could get married and ruin everything . . . '

The Fonsecas are people of their word,' ti Aureliano said reassuringly. 'Besides, who'd marry them? The older sisters are past it. The youngest has a pitted face. Teodolinda is thirty-eight. You're fifty. She's a good match, good looking. There are no male inheritors. The sisters will yield to the brother-in-law. What do you say?'

Franjoão bit his lip, chary of replying too soon.

'They're respectable people, you say?' he asked. 'Their family is a good one, but you never know . . . '

'Soledade's the man of the house. She's got quite a talent for managing the estate. On that score you can rest assured . . . '

'Do they still have the land in Divar?'

'Yes.'

'How many khandis of paddy a year?'

'Seven.'

'Coconuts?'

'Two thousand.'

'What else? Bananas, mangoes, jackfruit?'

'Those too. And they've got other lands.'

'Where?'

'In Dongrim.'

'What produce?'

'Rice. Various types. And lots of mangoes, over in Benaulim.'

'What about at home? Proper mangoes or just sucking ones?'

'You must be kidding? Good mango varieties, Xavier, Fernandina. A good family too. An old line of Brahmins, as you well know. Teodolinda gets the lot.'

'Really?'

'Of course. What they're after is a man of character, someone they'll get on with and who'll enhance the family's standing.'

Franjoão lowered his head and thought it over.

III

There was much to-ing and fro-ing between Margão and Saligão to set terms—always knotty when money is involved. Ti Aureliano proved tireless. All the same, one day, he had to get something off his chest: 'What on earth have I got myself into? My word, I've never seen a man more difficult to please. He wants to know everything down to the last detail: the harvests, the contents of the godown, the family jewels, the coffers . . . Please let it all work out. Don't let me come to regret this!'

But after all the trials and tribulations, the exchange of rings, the wedding ceremony and the tornaboda finally took place. Franjoão was unable to contain his enthusiasm: 'I'll be grateful to you as long as I live, ti Aureliano. It's to you that I owe my happiness.'

Happiness in his case was a mansion the size of an abbey stuffed with ancient china, inlaid cabinets, ivories, jewels, gemstones, thick gold bracelets, a well-stocked larder and acres of productive land. As for Teodolinda, she really was the best sister, though the freshness of youth had long faded from her cheeks.

The newlyweds honeymooned in British India, visiting Bombay, where Franjoão dipped into the nest egg he had put aside in Mozambique. He did so gladly, for times had changed. Gladly, that is, until he was presented with the bill. His bright idea of taking rooms at the Taj proved to be a costly one. Luckily, they only stayed a few days or he would have frittered away all the money he'd taken ten years to save up in Africa.

They also paid a visit to his new cousin Roberto Fonseca in Belgaum which ended up saving Franjoão's skin. Times had changed, but not too much, as he soon found out. They were away for a fortnight. Upon their return, Franjoão turned to his sisters-in-law, filled with enthusiasm for the new life he was about to begin, and declared: 'Tomorrow I shall go to Benaulim to inspect the land!'

Quick as a flash Soledade shot back: 'Don't trouble yourself, Franjoão. Everything is in hand. I was there not three days ago.'

'Really?' he exclaimed, rubbing his chin thoughtfully. 'Then I'll go to Divar to see the paddies.'

'Don't. There's no need. You should get some rest. So rest easy. I was there last week . . . '

'What about Dongrim?' he asked.

'There's nothing to do there now. Only next month, when the weeding begins . . . '

Franjoão shrugged and strode towards the door. He was just leaving when he spotted a large, sweet-smelling mango on the tabletop. He turned round, picked it up, weighed it in his hand and then began to peel back the skin.

'Mano Franjoão!' Claudina shrieked

He started, smearing his face with juice in the process.

'What? What is it? What happened?'

'You're eating the mango with your hands!'

'Of course, mana. How did you want me to eat it?'

Now Soledade intervened, wielding her authority as the eldest sister: 'Let me tell you, Franjoão, if the Barretos are a good family, the Fonsecas are not an inch behind. And in our house we always eat mangoes with cutlery. You'd better accustom yourself to our ways!'

Franjoão blushed. He wavered, unsure how to answer or react. But react he must. He stammered a few unintelligible words and then, in a gesture of helpless rage, hurled the half-peeled mango to the floor before stalking out of the room.

That night his wife said: 'Really, Franjoão. How could you offend my sisters like that?'

'I'm not a child,' he snapped, nose still out of joint. 'If I feel like eating a fruit with my hands, I'll do so! I had a bellyful of minding my Ps and Qs in Africa . . . '

'But you must behave, Franjoão!' Teodolinda answered tenderly. 'You know what the servants are like. Terrible gossips. Everyone would hear that we eat mangoes with our hands. We must keep up our good name, don't you see?'

Franjoão stared at her, open-mouthed. Then, honestly, he replied that yes, he did see.

'So you'll apologize to Soledade tomorrow?'

He muttered something inconclusive.

The next day, however, when he came down to breakfast, he found a tray of mangoes, small plates and cutlery on the table. He sat down in silence and began to eat, watching his sisters-in-law out of the corner of his eye. After he had finished, he hooked his thumbs through the waistband of his trousers and said, as if nothing had happened: 'I feel like lentil and jaggery pudding today!' Suddenly he felt four pairs of eyes trained upon him.

'What a notion, mano Franjoão!' Dejanira exclaimed. 'Lentil and jaggery!'

He was about to answer when Soledade nipped the conversation in the bud.

'Impossible. We're having ailé-belé for dessert!'

'Couldn't you leave that for tomorrow and make jagrada today, mana Soledade?' he ventured with the best of intentions.

'No!' she barked. 'I'm in charge of this house and you'd do well not to forget it, Franjoão!'

He tried to protest: 'But I . . . '

'This is women's business. Why don't you make half-a-dozen of those dhumtis for us to smoke later on? We've finished the others . . . '

A little while later Franjoão found himself shredding a plug of tobacco and rolling it up in banana leaves. How could a woman smoke these horrid dhumtis, he thought. They even made *him* cough. But Soledade—he had come to this conclusion already—was worse than a man. As he rolled the dhumtis and lined the finished products up on the lid of the leaf box, he recalled happy days spent in

Lourenço Marques, carousing in the Polana Hotel with cousin Miranda and Pascoalito Noronha, the quiet weekends in Namaacha, those fine whiskies cooled with ice, at night, in the Continental. The thought of whisky whetted his thirst. His sister-in-law was out back putting things away. He raised his head and shouted: 'Do you have any whisky in the house, mana Soledade?'

He heard her reply: 'What was that, mano Franjoão?'

'I asked if you had any whisky in the house!'

Soledade appeared at the door, her arms crossed.

'Yes, we do. What for?'

'Where is it?'

'Put away. Don't get any ideas, Franjoão. Whisky isn't for drinking. It's only for guests. We have our good name to think of, remember? And don't you lay a finger on the cheese and biscuits, do you hear? Just yesterday I saw you sniffing around the cupboard. They're for guests only . . . '

IV

Margão is a small town. A trading town of low houses, well-tended residences with gardens and fruit trees. It differs from Pangim—the bureaucratic capital—in its bustle and activity. Factories, emporia, export firms, all these give life in Margão a fast-paced rhythm that is a little surprising under these tropical skies. But in the antique houses of solid stone, darkened by time like convents, the old families don't relinquish their privileges. Time rolls on like an unchanging river which no obstacle can divert from its course. The old ways are obeyed, pride is maintained and arrogance preens itself.

Days, weeks, months, years mean nothing to the inhabitants of those venerable mansions; they have no truck with the parvenu shop-owners swanning around town and driving off to take the waters at Colvá in glistening new Chevrolets.

The life of the old bhatcars remains the same—unvarying, inalterable, centuries old, our daily rice wrested from the land by the sweat of our downtrodden mundcars' brows.

It didn't take Franjoão long to get used to his new situation. He began to smoke home-rolled dhumtis, to doze the afternoons away after stuffing himself with platefuls of curry and to eat mangoes with a knife and fork. He would drink a wee dram only when guests visited the house. The lack of whisky was, in fact, his biggest torment, especially on those long monsoon days when heavy downpours prevented him even from strolling in the garden . . . He would then resort to a little flask of urrak hidden in his pocket; he would swig from it on the sly. That raised his spirits and gave him an inner solace. Life spent this way didn't drag too much and he was filled with odd vital urges. Mana Soledade continued to run the household, to oversee the estates, to manage every instant of their lives.

Until one day, returning from a visit to mano Franxavier, who still lived modestly in their paternal home, Franjoão was met with a great outburst of joy. Teodolinda wasn't there. But ti Aureliano was, as were the three other sisters who crowded round with hysterical cries: 'Mano Franjoão, we have an heir! A successor to our line!'

He stepped back in bewilderment.

'An heir? What? What do you mean? I don't understand!'

'Yes, a successor . . . ' they cried.

His confusion lasted until ti Aureliano stepped forward and wrapped him in a tight embrace. 'A great day, Franjoão my friend, a great day for all of you in this house! I am so happy to have brought about such happiness. Imagine, I'd even been scared that things wouldn't work out! But everything has gone swimmingly. Congratulations, Franjoão my friend, you are going to be a father!'

Franjoão struggled free from the old man's scrawny arms and turned to face his sisters-in-law. He could still hardly believe it.

'Teodolinda . . . ?'

'Dr Noronha was here today. He says there can be no doubt!' Dejanira gasped, red-faced and breathless with excitement.

'Our grandfather Adeodato da Purificação do Santíssimo Sacramento Fonseca has returned to save our house!' Soledade intoned.

'Fonseca?' Franjoão stammered awkwardly. 'What about Barreto? Let's get one thing clear, mana Soledade. If it's a boy, and God willing it shall be, do you know whom he'll represent? My father, Francisco João dos Milagres Barreto!'

'Barreto?!' Soledade shrieked, standing on tiptoes, almost beside herself. 'Don't forget that you're a ghor-zavoim. Your child will be a FON-SE-CA and will have his maternal grandfather's name. One Franjoão in the family is enough.'

Franjoão lowered his head. He took out a dhumti and placed it pensively between his lips.

Dhruva

Dhruva sat facing East, pondering her fate. For the first time since the tali she felt a little scared. Until this point it had all been enchanting, a beautiful dream, but now she was afraid it would end. Now everything frightened her: the priest, the visitors who roamed freely through the house, her imperious, overpowering mother-in-law, her father-in-law, her kaku, everyone, even her husband . . . There had been that odd shiver when she'd felt Chandracanta's hands fasten the tali round her neck, knotting it three times. Yet this reaction came as a surprise. She could barely look this stranger who was now her husband in the eye, but was unable to find grounds for these feelings either. The laws had been obeyed and everything had taken place according to tradition. There had been nothing strange or different. She'd considered herself the luckiest girl in the village, she recalled, when her father announced the arrangement of her union with a son of the wealthy, influential house of Dessai, one of the best families in the district. She remembered too the day when she had decorated her long plait with jhele made from zaieu and abolim flowers to proclaim her betrothal to family and friends. She remembered it all, her parents' and her uncle's joy, all three contented yet nervous; the envy of the other girls her age who, when they saw her pass by so filled with happiness, would turn their backs; those magic days that preceded the tali . . . Her dreams, those tremulous hopes, all yielding to this feeling of disquiet before the unknown.

Although she was now permitted to look directly upon her husband, Dhruva sensed something immovable between them. It wasn't just the presence of guests all over the house; it wasn't just the mass of people crowding round them. It was something else, something more. Dhruva and Chandracanta exchanged only brief glances, occasional glances that drifted away and were lost among the visitors. They weren't able to find a moment to themselves, to exchange a word. Chandracanta's smile alone gave her encouragement and made her feel less alone. For Dhruva did feel alone, plucked suddenly from her own people to join another household. It was true that she felt secure, as secure as if she'd remained in her own home, and that she knew things had to be this way, yet she couldn't help but feel a deep saudade for her childhood room.

Dhruva bowed her head and considered herself fortunate; the Dessais were a good family. Besides, her sister Nalini had been wed even younger. She was only eleven when she joined the house of Camotim.

She now recalled all the bustle of that day and of the week that followed, the women of the house, the visitors who stayed for days on end, the whirl of people, and herself, always a smile on her face, eyes to the floor. And the gossip, filling the kitchen: 'Dhruva's jewels are all real', her mother-in-law repeated incessantly. 'Ei, suné! Dhruva-bai, come show your jewels to the family!'

And Dhruva promptly obeyed that nagging voice, taking her place amid the huddle of women, impassive under their searching, prying eyes. And afterwards, she had to explain the origin of each jewel: the pearls and the sapphires had come from her mother's side, the rubies from her father's, this thick bracelet had been a present from her kaku, these earrings had been bought . . . Ah, and her mother had worn the gold-embroidered sari on her own wedding day and then kept it especially for her.

On and on this went, again and again, interminably. What of Chandracanta . . . ? Almost ritually, at dinnertime, with her head bowed Dhruva would place the metal plates before her husband, her father-in-law, her grandfather and her uncle. When she reached Chandracanta she felt he looked not at his plate but at the hands that held it, her hands, the hands of a child. And Dhruva felt a strange tenderness burgeon and grow, and she would gaze down, so far down, at the face of her husband, her husband, her husband . . . Each time they crossed paths, and Chandracanta made as if to speak, inevitably at that very moment somebody would call out: 'Ei, Dhruva-bai! Ei, Chandracanta! Come over here, we have visitors. People from the village are here to meet the bride.'

And over they would go, smiling as a sign of amiability, yet holding their tongues, for only Chandracanta's parents and grandfather could speak, could relay the newlyweds' thoughts and desires.

All of this was normal, this was just how it was, in accordance with age-old customs, and though she felt strange qualms, Dhruva accepted everything as natural and was beginning to adapt to her new home. But what she didn't expect, what left her paralysed and gasping for breath, was to hear her father-in-law say to one of the visitors: 'It's a great honour for us all. When Chandracanta returns from Portugal, he will be a doctor!'

Dhruva felt a sudden dizziness. The only thing she understood was that her husband was going somewhere far away, far away, so very far away . . . and she saw rising before her mountains and valleys, plains, seas, an infinite distance between her and Chandracanta. But she couldn't be sad, no, she couldn't show herself to be sad, for this was good news, this was a sign of the family's happiness and contentment. She sought out her husband's face and felt the urge to shower him with questions . . . Why didn't he go instead to Bombay, which was so much closer? Why Portugal, a country that was so far off, so foreign? Portugal, for Dhruva, meant 'distance', 'separation' and, who knows, perhaps 'misunderstanding' after so many years apart . . .

She was roused from these thoughts by the harsh voice of her mother-in-law: 'Hey, Dhruva-bai, go and serve your father-in-law and your husband their food, you lazy girl! So much effort you put into making this xacuti! Everyone is awaiting the honour of you serving them . . . '

Dhruva bowed her head, picked up the metal plates and tiptoed into the dining room, where the men were sitting on the floor, talking among themselves. She approached slowly and, bending low, without looking at anyone, distributed the food. She felt her father-in-law observing her from the corner of his eye.

'See, I told you she would make an excellent house-wife!' he said to Chandracanta.

Dhruva merely smiled blankly.

The men lost no time in sampling the young daughter-in-law's xacuti.

'What's this, you're not eating?' Chandracanta's father asked, patting him gently on the shoulder. 'You shouldn't worry about Dhruva. We'll be here to watch over her . . . You know very well that it's in your best interest that she, and all of us, should make this sacrifice. What an honour for our family if you become a doctor!'

But Chandracanta's grandfather didn't see things in this light. Why should his grandson go so far away, just to become a doctor? Weren't they merchants held in high regard, who wielded great influence? 'Vah va!' he cleared his throat noisily, expressing his displeasure:

A hint of unease passed over every face, for they knew that was Apai's characteristic way of deriding someone.

'Why vah va? Is it not an honour to become a doctor?'

'Vah va!' repeated the old man, getting slowly to his feet and stretching his arms and legs.

Dhruva could no longer contain herself. She hid her face with her palov, so no one could see the tears brimming in her eyes, and ran from the room.

Distressed at this turn of events, Chandracanta also took the opportunity to get up from his seat. He quickly crossed the central courtyard, then stopped at the end of a corridor to peer into the gloom.

'Dhruva!' he whispered. 'Dhruva!'

To his left, he seemed to hear the muffled sound of crying. Anxiously he turned.

'Dhruva!' he repeated. 'Is that you?'

He took a couple of slow steps along the darkened corridor.

'Dhruva! Dhruva!'

The faint light of a divtti helped him find his bearings. He stopped and hesitated by the doorway. There she lay huddled and unmoving upon a divan. Shyly, he approached. He gave the hem of her sari a gentle tug and then, as if his strength had failed, fell to his knees beside her and kissed her softly on the cheek.

'Are you crying, Dhruva? Aren't you happy in my parents' house?' he whispered, and then began to sob, resting his head against her breast.

Dhruva was alarmed by this unexpected display. At heart, she'd expected Chandracanta to show an attitude that would instil respect, exert his authority as her husband. She ran her fingers through his hair.

'Chand, what's wrong? Chand, are you really going to leave?'

'Yes, but I shall return. And you'll always be my Dhruva to guide my journey. You know what Dhruva means, don't you, Dhruva? Dhruva is the Pole Star, and means faithful, steadfast. I'll go, but I'll be back, Dhruva, my little girl, my little Pole Star . . . '

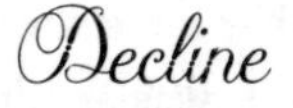

Grandmother had become a symbol. In life, she'd been respected by the whole family. The mundcars had worshipped her as a providential idol, as a protector. Even after her death, she continued to influence our every action. It was she, always she, who from even beyond the grave would continue to direct our lives.

For many years an ill dread gripped my mother, that the flame her own had kindled within us might fizzle out. Whenever one of us wavered before the enigmas of this world, she would say in hope: 'May your grandmother guide you, my children!'

These words, intoned almost religiously, roused us like a magic potion and took us back to the old Brahmin traditions so hallowed in our family. In a flash, Grandmother returned to life. Once more we could see her in the dining room, confidently and serenely directing the servants from her armchair, or out on the land, overseeing the harvest, watching on as the mundcars, heads bowed, stocked coconuts in our godown.

When Grandmother sat at the head of the long table and presided over tea, it was an almost religious experience. She taught us to take our drinks calmly, in small, silent sips. Any visitor dropping by was invited to take part in the ceremony, though his presence wouldn't bring the slightest change to the ritual.

When my brothers or I went to the house of a relative, in Mapuçá, in Badém or in Pangim, Grandmother would always recommend discretion. She knew that adults often used children to pry into other people's lives.

' "I don't know" is the best answer if they're too nosy,' she would say with a contemptuous smile.

The sudden death of our father in Africa had laid Grandmother low. You could say that from that day on she began to grow old, as if on purpose.

'This house is finished!' she would repeat endlessly in the altar room where she spent most of her time at prayer, her eyes fixed on the Sacred Heart of Jesus.

'How can our house be finished, Mai?' Roberto would ask, from the height of his ten meagre years.

'I can't explain that to you now . . . ' our mother would reply in a frail voice, as frail as her defenceless female frame. 'When you grow up, baba . . . '

The first year after our father's death brought no alteration to our family routine. All the changes began when, immediately after the monsoon, death bore off the one irreplaceable member of our family—Grandmother passed away!

I don't recall the details of the stroke that made her relinquish her duties for good. I only know that when she died, the ancestral flame did too.

'Mother's death is a catastrophe!' my own exclaimed, flailing desperately for something to cling to. But all she found were the panicked faces of her four children.

Belinda's fourteen years were too few for her to gauge the terrible situation in which we found ourselves. Roberto, who was two years younger, was no more able either. Lena and I, the youngest, could do nothing but weep.

The heavy crystal chandelier drizzling light, the glistening silverware, the ancient china heaped on the sideboard and hanging from the walls, the ponderous furniture —these were the only witnesses to our catastrophe. Amid these age-old objects lay Grandmother's lifeless body. It was the end of an era.

The mundcars sensed this end sooner than one might imagine. They came slowly, in silence, lost now that the estate to which they'd belonged for so many generations had collapsed. They entered the room, huddling together as if for protection, and stared. One by one, shy yet emboldened, they started to occupy the chairs ranged before the bier. In loud voices they prayed: *Amchea bapa, tum sorgar assai . . .* —Our Father, who art in heaven . . .

Directly she spotted them, Belinda came running: 'Mama! Mama!' she cried indignantly.

'Don't shriek like that, baiee, while the body of your grandmother lies in this house!' warned our mother, bedridden since the day before.

'Mama! The mundcars . . . '

'Don't tell me there's been another disaster!' she whispered, shutting her tearful eyes.

'The mundcars sat on the chairs!' my sister informed her, in a voice full of heartfelt indignation.

'The mundcars *sat down*? Lord, where will I find the courage to bear such humiliation,' our mother stammered, slumping back.

My little brother, who was at her bedside, exclaimed instinctively: 'I shall go and forbid them to remain seated!'

'No, my son! It'd be far worse if they disobeyed . . . '

'But they'd have never dared while Grandmother was alive . . . the mundcars kept their distance when she spoke to them!'

Helped by Belinda, Mother sat up in bed and began to speak in a low voice. Though at times a jumbled murmur, some of her words would be engraved in our memory forever. Yet only much later, after many years had passed and life had punished us severely, did we fully understand their meaning.

'We cannot avoid this catastrophe. I know they don't see me as the foundation needed for this house to survive . . . .They only see the fragile woman that I am. I have never been able to handle them like your grandmother, though she tried to show me the ropes of the estate. What they need is someone who commands them, who gives them confidence in the future and I . . . I'm no more than a defenceless bhatcan!'

She fell silent and hesitated. The glimmer in her eyes reminded us momentarily of Grandmother. She pulled Roberto's small, frail body to her and exclaimed with a burst of vigour: 'Four women now depend on you, baba! Four women, the land, and eighty mundcars whose futures lie in your hands and who need your guidance. A great responsibility rests on your shoulders, my son. You are a great bhatcar, never forget that, baba! Your grandmother has faith in you!'

My brother bowed his head, as if crushed by the weight of his inheritance, and gave no answer.

'You'll understand, baba. One day, you'll understand. But it'll take time, and on that day the mundcars shan't sit on the chairs of our house . . . '

But all of us, and my brother too, felt that my mother no longer believed. And to go on you have to believe.

Hope

Outside the rain fell in fat drops, soaking the earth. Through the low roof came thin streams of water which dripped monotonously onto the packed-dung floor. Crouching by the threshold, quite still, Pedru stared out at the river. Before him the landscape was blurred by a liquid curtain. Besides the water pouring from the sky, the only sound was from the scraping stone his sister used to grind the masala, an equally doleful noise. Their mother, squatting in a corner, grumbled under her breath. Pedru couldn't make out the words. He remained silent, and gazed at the roiling current. Now and then a stronger gust of wind blew spray into the house.

'Close the door, Pedru!' muttered his mother. 'It's cold!'

'But it's stifling in here!' the boy replied as he bent forward.

'It is stifling,' said the old woman, echoing his words. 'But not from heat . . . '

They fell silent.

These were the first rains of the monsoon, which forced everyone to stay inside. Pedru shook his head dejectedly.

'Do you think I should go, Mai?'

'Go where, Pedru?'

'To speak to Mitzi-baiee!'

The old woman didn't answer. Morgorit went on grinding the masala as if nothing else mattered. Suddenly, however, the sound of the stone ceased.

'As soon as there's a break in the weather, you should go and fetch some olas for the roof," the girl said. 'The churtas are coming apart and letting rain through.'

Pedru said nothing. It was his mother who replied in an indignant voice.

'Alalala, Morgorit! Pedru can't spend his time out there fixing the roof. He went to the Liceu so he could get a good job . . . '

'Hus!' the girl exclaimed. 'I'm fed up with working while Pedru sits around all day earning nothing . . . '

'He doesn't want to come to the paddy with us, Morgorit,' the old woman insisted. 'He wants to get a government post.'

The girl fell silent. The scraping of the stone was heard once more. A little while later, she spoke again: 'I've been working, haven't I, Mother? I worked from dawn till dusk so that Pedru could study at the Liceu. I've worked for years without complaint so that Pedru could be someone important like Robert-bab. But now Pedru can't get a job and I'm still working because he can't come to the paddy. Is that fair, mother? Ay, kata-kata! I've no dowry and have to go on working so that Pedru can stay at home smoking bidis. How much longer, Mother?'

Over in her corner the old woman squirmed. She understood her daughter's point of view. She understood that she was right. But making this sacrifice for Pedru was worth it. He would surely get a job. He was a smart lad. Just a little more patience . . .

She leant over and tapped her son on the shoulder. The boy started, averting his eyes momentarily from the rain outside.

'Go! Go and speak to Mitzi-baiee, Pedru. Go and speak to her. She's a good bhatcan. She'll help you.'

'But they're poor, Mother. As poor as us. What can they do? Vitol's wife Mogrém was there a few days back and saw them having only apas and tea for lunch! They're poorer than we are, mother. Do you really think Mitzi-baiee could . . . ?'

The old lady slowly fingered a dhumti before placing it between her lips. Then she lit up and took a puff.

'But they're Brahmins, Pedru. Ancient Brahmins. Poor or not it doesn't matter. All top people of Pangim they know. Their relatives work in the government. Cousins of all the important people, people with influence. They're poor now, but once they were the grandest bhatcars in Orlim. I still remember seeing Teresin-bai in the big house, in beautiful dresses, receiving the paclé. And her mother, Rogin-bai, a great bhatkan. Very generous. In her time, no one went hungry in Orlim. There was rice and coconuts for everyone. Her godown was open to anyone in need. It was their ruin. And the balls they gave too. Balls that lasted four days. Everyone from the government came, even the governor. When I was a girl, I worked in her grandmother's kitchen. And her father . . . a handsome man! Robert-bab is the spitting image, though without his character . . . no, but he's a good boy . . . . When their father died, they began selling everything off. The grandmother died, and now they are poorer than we are. You're right, but don't you see that they're still our bhatcars? Everybody respects them still because they're good bhatcars. Nothing like bhatcar Dias who scrapes the skin off our bones and only leaves our soul because it belongs to God . . . '

Pedru licked the rain the wind brought in from his lips.

The old woman continued: 'Let's pray the rosary, Pedru, so that Mitzi-baiee might find you a job. The sacrifices we both made for your schooling shall be rewarded. Remember that you're the first from Orlim to attend the Liceu. That should fill us with pride. All our sacrifices were worth it, weren't they, Morgorit? Let's say three Our Fathers for old Rogin-baiee, may she rest in the peace of the Lord . . . *Amchea bapa, tum sorgar . . .* '

A loud burst of thunder drowned out the words. Through the churtas of the roof, thicker drops of rain began to drip.

* * *

'At the last minute he springs this on us!' Mitzi exclaimed. 'Now Roberto's saying he doesn't want to come, Mother . . . '

Teresa smiled and looked at her son.

'Go on, Roberto, you must accompany your sisters. Don't you see they must find a match?'

Mitzi, golden-skinned and nineteen years old, was furious.

'We're going to miss the best do at the Clube Nacional and all because of him. After all the money I've spent on this dress! What a rotten trick to play on us. It's just not fair, Mother!'

'All they do is dance with the paclé and my friends see and pass comment,' Roberto yelled, angry in turn. 'They're both crazy . . . '

'Pay no attention, Mother. I only dance with them now and again. Lena dances more. But what's wrong with that? Look,' she said, turning to her brother, 'It'll be your loss if you miss out on the buffet. They say this year's is better than ever . . . '

Roberto went over and set himself in a *cadeira voltaire*. He rocked back and forth, not looking at Mitzi.

'Lena's just gone over to see ti Jerónima, who's a dab hand with hair. When she gets back, she's going to be furious, I can tell you . . . '

Roberto went on rocking and gave no answer. Their mother had gone out to the back of the house and the two siblings were now alone. Mitzi glanced over at her brother's serious face. Then she walked towards him and sat on the floor by his side. The boy didn't move, pretending not to have noticed. She took his hand and began to stroke it.

'Do you remember when Grandmother died, Roberto?' she asked. 'You're right, it left us in a bad way. We have to be very careful if we're to save the family name, you're right. I know full well that people are watching, just waiting for us to make a wrong move so they can laugh at our expense. I know well how awfully difficult it is for poor girls with no father to evade gossip. But we're sensible girls and we've got you, the very best of brothers. Right, shall we stay at home tonight? How about a game of cards, Roberto? Let's invite cousin Alzira over. We'll have a blast!'

Roberto stared at his sister in surprise, unsure what she was up to.

'Well, I . . . that wasn't exactly what I meant. I just hate it when you dance with the paclé. Why don't you just dance with our boys? Those paclé have no morals and give girls a bad name, as you well know!'

'You're quite right,' Mitzi answered gravely. 'Our boys are so different from the paclé. Do you think I'd ever marry a European? Besides, they might cut a dash here, but over there they're nothing. And stupid too, haven't you noticed? Our boys are very different. Marriage is for life. *They* swap women like they change their shirts . . . I'd rather marry a Shudra than a paclo! Ah, on the subject of Shudras, do you know who came here earlier to ask us to find him a job? Pedru. Just picture it! Yes, Pedru, the son of Salubrancar, Salu who likes white wine! Those people are becoming unbearable. Now that he's been to the Liceu, he thinks he's someone and wants a job. They think they're our equals. Whatever next? He turned up here with lots of baiee-faiee, addressing me as if we were of his ilk. I put him in his place. He wanted me to ask cousin Josinho to get him a job in the finance department. Whatever next? His mother and sister out there in the paddy and he thinks he's a bigwig just because he went to the Liceu. He's got some cheek, don't you think?'

Roberto nodded solemnly in agreement, then turned to his sister: 'Right, be off and get ready. You still want to go to the dance, don't you? When's Lena back?'

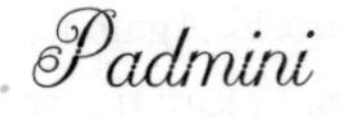

Padmini

Ganesh was just around the corner, and Pangim almost ready to celebrate. People had flocked in from all over, even from the Indian Union, filling the streets and shops with colourful fabrics. Dark-skinned men in loincloths strode the marketplaces; slender women in garish saris, their arms laden with gold bracelets, scarlet kumkum on their foreheads, adorned themselves with garlands of zaieus and bought sweet treats. Transformed into an outlandish watercolour, Pangim found itself immersed in the heady scents of betel and chondor-vatt.

With a laugh, Lieutenant Gama turned to João Fidalgo: 'Why don't you drop in at Sirvoicar's to see Ganesh? It's a golden opportunity to see your lotus flower again.'

João Fidalgo shook his head wryly and regarded his friend.

'You don't really think I can go to Sirvoicar's?'

'Why not?' the other answered with a suggestive grin.

João Fidalgo remembered that morning, so distant now, when he had boarded the ship for India filled with visions of a different world. Again he saw the slim, nervous boy who appeared just before the vessel weighed anchor.

'Captain Fidalgo? Sir, are you Captain Fidalgo?'

The boy stuttered and stumbled inarticulately over his words, all the while darting glances up at the ship where waving soldiers filled the bows. Dr Fidalgo (João's uncle, a lecturer at the Medical School) had told the boy to seek out his nephew before he embarked. It was just a little something. A small gift for the boy's father and sister. Would he mind taking it to them?

Afterwards, as the ship moved off, João Fidalgo watched the thin, swarthy figure of the boy standing stiffly on the dockside. Gradually it sank back, leaving only the whitish smear of the dissolving city.

João Fidalgo remembered all this and his anguish months later when he found the package forgotten in a previously unopened suitcase. Bewildered by his first contact with that strange land, he'd completely forgotten the Hindu boy who'd handed it to him as he left. 'It's just a small gift for my father and my sister . . . '

And, in his eyes, a timeless nostalgia.

Almost three months later, João Fidalgo had found himself clutching that package again, unsure what to do: 'Dr Sirvoicar, Rua Cunha Rivara, Pangim.'

It all came back to him now, filling João Fidalgo's mind. Dr Sirvoicar, spruce in a brilliant white puddvem, and the hypnotic black eyes of . . .

'Padmini!' Sirvoicar had said, anticipating his question.

He had spoken almost brusquely, even anxiously, as if in fear of some impending catastrophe.

'Padmini!' he repeated. 'It means "lotus woman"!'

Sirvoicar paused, as if scrutinizing João Fidalgo's soul, before gazing out at the vast mango tree in the garden.

'Padmini, the fourth and final stage of the female soul ere it merges into Brahma!'

He would've liked to hear her voice, even only a simple whispered 'bom dia'. But Padmini's voice was a smile. Just a smile. One so different, so profound, so intimate even, that it left him feeling self-conscious, unsure what to do with his hands and eyes. Any other girl would have addressed him confidently: 'It's a pleasure to have you here with us' or some such phrase. Padmini merely smiled. 'A timeless smile,' João Fidalgo thought. 'As old and sacred as their animal-shaped idols . . . '

And Gama reminding him of it all with unwitting cruelty: 'Why don't you drop by Sirvoicar's to see Ganesh? It's a golden opportunity . . . '

'Lotus-woman wrapped in a white sari, flowers in her long hair . . . ' thought João Fidalgo, recalling those slow, baking afternoons in the *irani* at the end of the street, from where one could see the dirty walls of Sirvoicar's house, a quiet and unassailable fortress. He was surprised at himself for thinking 'Sirvoicar's house' and not 'Padmini's house'. Sirvoicar's house, as old and dark as the scorched earth he walked on. He remembered the afternoons of anxious waiting. Sometimes he felt so ridiculously sentimental that he would throw his head back and laugh hysterically.

He was like some moustachioed Romantic from the nineteenth century, gazing at his beloved from afar, pining for the briefest glance, as short-lived as the scalding tea. that slaked his thirst and drugged his senses . . . He recalled the *irani* and the little Hindu lad who'd served him. The *irani*, his observation post, and the pointless, unredeemed times he sat in wait, sipping that hot tea, so aromatic and refreshing . . .

'It's a golden opportunity to see your lotus flower again,' Lieutenant Gama repeated, in his bluff, ironic manner.

"You don't really think I can go to Sirvoicar's?'

'Why not?'

João Fidalgo turned away.

'Hey, if you want to, you don't need an invitation! It's the feast of Ganesh!'

With a sort of quizzical glance, he went on: 'But watch your step, pal! You're still a greenhorn here in India. If you think you can have your way with the lass, you can forget it, let me tell you! Hindu girls don't marry our lot. The parents arrange their marriages and only with men from the same caste. Courting like you did in Lisbon? Not a chance. See you get that into your thick head, right?'

'Do you mean . . . ?' João Fidalgo's voice trailed away.

'I mean,' Lieutenant Gama said with feeling, 'I mean that we haven't a hope with the local girls. Apart from the tarts, of course, tarts are the same everywhere, only good to pass the time. The thing is the others are so mouth-watering . . . '

They had walked almost the whole of Campal. Finding a bench, they sat down. João Fidalgo hung his head.

'You're right,' he murmured. 'With Padmini it was different. And look, I've known some women. But Padmini . . . She was serene, thoughtful. All I felt was tenderness and respect . . .'

'Of course. It happens to us all. Some take a while, others get it straight away. But sooner or later we all realize these people have roots and customs we must accept . . . and respect!'

The sun sank swiftly towards the horizon. João Fidalgo rose to his feet.

'Off to see Ganesh then?' asked his friend.

'No! Listen, you told me nothing new . . . I saw it on Sirvoicar's face. When I tried to speak to Padmini, he stepped in and answered for her, raising an impenetrable barrier between the two of us. He noticed something in my tone of voice, the glint in my eyes. I don't know . . . He stepped in as if wanting to avert a sacrilege. He even managed to stop her telling me her own name . . . '

'So you two never spoke?'

'No!' João Fidalgo replied. 'It was Sirvoicar who did all the talking. I never even heard her voice. . . '

The Future and the Past

It happened when the lotação—the bus in Brazil—sped into the tunnel and its lights didn't switch on for some odd reason.

Carlos Siqueira stared out through the windscreen. All he could see was a white spot in the distance, which began to expand rapidly . . . . It was, without doubt, the other end of the tunnel, which led out onto Avenida Princesa Isabel, but at that moment this fact escaped him. All he could see was a tiny white spot in the distance, on the far side of the darkness, growing ever larger. Of course, nothing strange or special was happening. He must have had the same experience on other occasions, but this time, due to his particular state of mind, it sent him tumbling back into the past.

Already that very morning in the office, without knowing why, Carlos Siqueira had recalled the village of his birth. The memory had come suddenly and overpoweringly, but he'd shaken his head and focused on the paperwork before him. It wasn't long, however, before his pen stopped moving and his gaze drifted to the blank wall opposite. The fact was he couldn't remember much about his village, but at that moment the life that had followed the day he left his parents' ancient home swept through his mind. Briefly, he thought back to those hard times in Nairobi, his pitiless exploitation of the blacks, all in the hope of returning home one day, doing up the family pile, providing dowries for his sisters, of living out his years on his native soil . . . He thought back to the total collapse of his dreams, his jarring defeats, his flight to Lourenço Marques, and from there to America, New York, Los Angeles. . . . Caroline! Carlos Siqueira snapped out of it and got back to work. He had no time for sentimentality. The past was over. Only the future mattered. Mattered to him.

The entrance of his partner Menezes interrupted his thoughts and impeded their analysis. For forty-five years he'd acted the same way, forging ahead without looking back, crushing everything in his path. In moments of loneliness, when he was forced to confront himself honestly, such as when Caroline died in that accident on 53rd Street, vague, disjointed images would come to him, from afar, from deep inside. But Carlos Siqueira pushed them away, screened them behind more pressing concerns. For almost forty-five years he had laid waste to the past. But on this day, when the lotação sped into that tunnel and its lights didn't turn on, the past came to him. That tiny spot began to dilate, to swell and occupy his mind. When the bus shot out onto Princesa Isabel and turned off towards Avenida Barata Ribeiro, the light outside hit him squarely in the eyes, dazzling him and unexpectedly shutting off the future, a vision of which he had sought desperately to counteract his newly awoken memories.

Carlos Siqueira experienced a feeling of utter defeat. That future, his future, his here and now, had nothing to do with the future of the Carlos Siqueira who'd left Goa over forty years ago with a bundle of clearly defined ambitions. Deep down inside, he felt that he'd failed, that he'd sold out his old hopes for nothing at all . . . He had forsaken everything, his past, even his own future. He had forgotten his family home, the old village, his sisters who must have waited year after year for the dowry he'd promised them . . . It had all been abandoned, even the future he'd once dreamt of. And all for what? All for . . .

Carlos Siqueira rose mechanically. The bus had reached his stop on Copacabana. He stepped down as he did each day and walked slowly off along the pavement.

He desperately wanted to be in Goa, to see his old house again . . . Forty-five years! His old house . . . his sisters . . . still unwed. He could go back to the future he'd once dreamt of. He could return. Money was no issue. He would simply appear, wave a wand, and make everyone happy. He would furbish the old house, give his sisters money, he would . . . he didn't know . . . he no longer knew what he would do! And suddenly it was he who was trying to remember, who was trying to summon back the past. He strove to recall the old house, the potholed roads of his village, the sad-faced mundcars, the Curumbins and their happy songs . . .What use was his wealth, what point importance in a land that wasn't his own, with no one there he'd played with as a child? He tried to summon the past, but it didn't answer. All that came were faded impressions that left him disappointed.

He trudged up the stairs. For the first time in his life he felt old, his sixty-seven years a sudden weight on his shoulders. He put his key in the lock. The mulatto maid ran out to meet him.

'Mistah Siqueira, someone on the phone for you. I was gonna say you was out when I heard the door.'

Carlos Siqueira nodded and picked up the handset.

'Is that you, Siqueira?' he heard Menezes rasp hurriedly. 'Listen up, pal, I'm here with Leopoldino, you know, that guy from Curitiba. Remember that undeveloped plot we saw three months back in Jacarepaguá? The one we wanted to buy? Well, Leopoldino wants to sell up and is only asking 9 million! D'you remember the figures we worked out, Siqueira? In four or five years, it'll be worth twenty big ones at least. It's a sweet deal. A once-in-a-lifetime opportunity! You got yourself one helluva partner, Siqueira. It's a sweet deal. Shall I buy it?'

'Buy it!' barked Siqueira before ringing off.

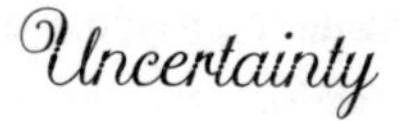

But Sousa didn't quite get Olavo Silva's hurry. Perhaps Mello himself had made the suggestion and was using him as a go-between. As it happened, they'd already discussed possible matches for Angélica, such as Álvares, Costa Pinto, even Mello himself. Of course they all came from good, well-connected families, with property. But you could never be sure of anything. Of course these families had respectable names, but, sometimes, when the time came for daughters to marry, they found artful ways to disguise their poverty and conceal their misfortunes so as not to spoil the chances of finding a suitable match. No father can rest easy until he's married his daughters into a good family and set them up for life. It was shameful for a daughter to go unwed. Worse still was starting negotiations only to have the proposal rejected.

Therefore he remained wary, often shutting his eyes and slyly playing for time. Meanwhile he thought things over, assessed the wiles of the go-between who often connived with the other party to present unlikely scenarios.

But the fact was that he'd delayed, put matters off in the hope of finding a catch for his daughter, and couldn't now let another opportunity slip through his fingers. So he had steeled himself and sought out his friend.

'In our neck of the woods, eh?' Olavo Silva exclaimed.

Children ran through the house, excited by the visit, and crept up to peep through the door.

Silva knew the reason behind that unexpected visit and got straight to the point. As he arranged the papers and documents scattered across his desk, he asked with an enthusiastic yet confidential air: 'You want to marry off your daughter, don't you?'

He got straight to the point so Sousa couldn't back out.

'Mello is a good prospect, wouldn't you say? I have it from a trustworthy source that he wants a wife. But he'll not be easy to convince. Seeks guarantees. I know him well. He's looking out for himself, of course. There are families with unwed daughters who are desperate to land him.'

He wiped his brow as though striving to weigh up the situation.

'Tell me, how much in dowry? He'll want to know, you understand.'

Sousa wasn't to be caught out. He heard a noise at the door and saw the maid had entered with two drinks. Spotting his chance, he coughed for a moment as though something were stuck in his throat.

'It's a good dowry, rest assured. But the dowry isn't the only thing. Angélica has other assets. As you know, she took piano classes! She's a fine housekeeper too. She isn't the kind who marries just to become a mother.'

'Now perhaps! Later, when women start having children, they forget about all that. The only sure thing is the dowry,' Silva remarked, trying to play down the piano lessons.

'She's not even that keen to get married', Sousa countered, trying to secure a bargaining position.

And, since the other man had raised his arm in a gesture of doubt, he hastened to add: 'Of course that isn't the problem. She must marry to preserve the family's reputation. A single girl . . . Well, I don't know if you see . . . '

'Naturally!' the other interrupted, shaking his head. 'But Mello will demand a good dowry. I'd like to know exactly how much you're offering. Because he's already drawing up a list. Mello looks out for himself, you know how things are! But if your daughter's dowry is a tidy amount, it wouldn't surprise me one bit if he accepted your offer.'

Sousa lost his patience, scowled and shouted: 'I'm a rich man and my daughter shall have a very respectable dowry. Will you take him my proposal or not?'

'Yes, yes, of course! And this afternoon I'll drop by your house with the answer you're looking for.'

Upon leaving, Sousa was plagued by a host of nagging doubts. He had the impression that somehow important questions had gone unbroached. He wanted to go back over everything with a fine-tooth comb, but, when he looked up at the clock, he saw that it was lunch time already: 'Delfina will be hopping mad I'm late,' he thought, quickening his step.

When he arrived home, there was a car parked at the front door. With a feeling of relief he saw that it was Silva there waiting. But Silva hurriedly said that he'd only stay a moment and that he needed just a few more concrete details . . . he needed to know whether the marriage contract would include the communion of assets.

'What! It'll be with separation of assets! What's he after?' Sousa asked, still wary.

'In that case we might as well stop here. Mello won't accept a wedding contract without a communion of assets!'

Sousa's wife lost her patience and burst into the room, hoping to salvage the situation.

'They say Mello draws a good salary. What's more, his family is rich and owns property.'

Sousa turned to his wife and replied firmly: 'Yes? But remember that what's at stake here is the dowry of our daughter Angélica. My only condition is the separation of assets.'

Olavo Silva fell silent. He was a little hesitant, but not about to yield. He glanced at his watch and tried to reprise his part as hurried go-between.

'I'm sorry but I can't stay any longer. Think it over and then let me know. How about another candidate besides Mello?'

It had started to rain. The drops beat loudly against the windows. These were early days; there would be a long wait yet until a good match was found.

Tiatr

The performance had already started by the time Bhatcar Dias and his wife arrived. They had got there late by design, to flaunt their rank. The great and the good suit themselves and Dias couldn't miss the chance to hammer that fact home. Besides, he was sure two places would be kept for them up at the front, to watch the show at their convenience. His wife Dona Serafina, for her part, would have come much earlier, to have a good look round and chitchat with the womenfolk. But she understood her husband's thinking. It wouldn't do to go soft, for those mundcars were getting uppity. Who knows what might happen if they weren't shown their place? The world was topsy-turvy, at sixes and sevens, and it wouldn't be long before mundcars and bhatcars were all lumped together. But not while he, Inácio Dias, was around, of that you could be sure. There were no improprieties on his estate. You are you, I am I, everything in its rightful place. Any time a barefaced Bomboicar showed up all hoity-toity, dressed in coat and trousers, ashamed to wear a langotim, his hair all slicked back, out he went. The bhatcar wasn't standing for that nonsense. Dung beetles don't stay in the dung, aanh? He well knew how they lived up there, fifteen or twenty to a room, like ants, saving up, squirrelling away so they could come back down to Goa and strut around like bigwigs. He, Inácio Dias, the greatest bhatcar in Orlim, was having none of it. No matter how much brilliantine they put in their hair, for him they were still his mundcars, or the sons of his mundcars, Severin, Xaiér, Antu . . .

You had to keep a grip, not let yourself get swept away. That's why he got there late. 'The great and the good suit themselves,' he said to his wife. But upon arriving he frowned, smelling a rat. He couldn't shilly-shally now though; he had his rank and couldn't back down. He took his wife by the arm and made his way into the crowd. He pushed and jostled, stuck in a hand, a knee, but made little headway. He could feel passive resistance all around, a collective determination not to let them pass. All of a sudden, he heard a yell: 'Hoy!'

Nonplussed, he turned his head and tried to identify the speaker. From the other side someone else shouted: 'Hus!'

He stared straight ahead, tense, distrustful. Another, disguised, voice cried out: 'If you want to stand, go to the back!'

He tried once again to put a face to the heckler. But how, amid such a crowd? Furious, he gesticulated and jostled his wife who, despite everything, was peering over at the stage, trying to follow the performance. Dona Serafina loved tiatr. Especially the spicy bits, when they acted out village gossip, the sly deals, the drunken sprees, the wrangling over inheritances, everything. Sometimes there were funny skits, like that of Paulu, whose wife had run off with a rickshaw driver and left him with four kids. Every year Paulu played himself in the tiatr, getting up and denouncing his wife. One year she'd even watched the performance. What shamelessness!

Dona Serafina loved tiatr. Her husband, however, was beside himself. Dona Serafina knew he was right. But couldn't he show a little patience? Bhatcar Dias was about to blow a gasket. How dare his mundcars? His *own* mundcars! They should've come out to greet him, all of them, actors too, all his mundcars together. Unable to control himself, he elbowed his wife and exclaimed: 'This is too much, Serafina! Let's go before this gets out of hand! . . . I'll have it out with Gustin tomorrow!'

Dona Serafina was disappointed by her husband's attitude. She didn't want to go home without seeing the tiatr. She had so few distractions. But she couldn't disagree with him. Whoever heard of a bhatcar receiving such treatment? Inácio was absolutely right, no doubt about it. They had to reassert themselves then and there and the seemliest way to do that was to withdraw immediately. Yet she thought it a great shame to miss this free tiatr. Besides, it was only on once a year. A barrel of laughs it was too, as the actors were all mundcars of theirs, village folk they'd known for years.

She turned to her husband: 'Inácio, why don't you have a word with Gustin? They say he's the organizer. Perhaps he doesn't know we've arrived!'

'Me, have a word with Gustin? Not a chance! He's an actor today, but tomorrow he'll be one of our mundcars again . . . then we'll see! Oh yes!'

He was about to continue his rant against Gustin when the band struck up anew. The curtain rose once more and Dona Serafina stood on tiptoe so she could see the stage.

'Look, there's Gustin, Motí, Pedru . . . . who's that other one? Looks like Venctexa.'

But her husband was still nettled. He muttered to his wife under his breath: 'Look how full of themselves they are! Not a tanga to their names, but togged up in those dinner jackets, anyone would take them for gentlemen!'

Absorbed in the melody and the lyrics of the song, and with trying to find a more comfortable position without anyone making a fuss, Dona Serafina replied innocently: 'But how do you want them to dress on stage? You didn't expect them to come out in loincloths?'

Her husband stared at her goggle-eyed, uncomprehendingly. But, suddenly, Gustin's voice rang out, and she turned to listen:

Porzollite tujim vhadd kam
Distat sorguinchem nekhetram
Tuca Dona Ana nomoscar kortaum
Anim ani soglo Orlieche gamv.

So brilliant were your deeds
Like stars in the sky
Please Dona Ana, accept our praise from us
And the whole village of Orlim.

Bhatcar Dias flinched, and his irritation went up a notch. Why were they always singing the praises of Dona

Ana, who had died more than a century ago? The bhatcar, and now Dona Serafina too, felt deeply offended. What were their mundcars thinking? It was his praises they should sing. The land they lived on belonged to him!

'Will they never forget Dona Ana? Every year a song in Dona Ana's honour. I'm getting fed up with Dona bloody Ana!'

'Whatever could she have done for these people to remember her so?,' Dona Serafina asked. Full of curiosity, as she was every year at the tiatr, she insisted: 'Inacinho, what was it Dona Ana did?'

Though he knew how forgetful his wife was, he was irked to have to explain it all yet again: 'Good grief, how many times do I have to tell you! Dona Ana was a benefactress of Orlim. She left some money to the confraria.'

Seeing that the song had finished, he nudged his wife, signalling that they should leave so as to avoid a new shower of protests. Disgruntled, Dona Serafina followed her husband into the crowd. They threaded their way through until they were nearly clear. Stepping free, they took a deep breath.

'Blast! What riff-raff!' Inácio Dias exclaimed, humiliated. But as he turned his head he found himself face-to-face with Gustin who stood drinking next to the soda vendor. Dias scowled.

Unable to escape, Gustin bowed his head in respect.

'Here to see our tiatr, bhatcar and bhatcarina?' he inquired humbly.

'We came as a courtesy to you!' the bhatcar exclaimed furiously. 'Didn't you know to keep two chairs for us at the front?'

'It's true. Bhatcarina, please forgive us . . . The chairs were needed for the musicians.'

Given such a plausible excuse, Dona Serafina tried to resolve things in her interest—staying and watching the tiatr—and replied in a friendly voice: 'Well, find us a bench at least. We shan't stay till the end.'

'A bench? I'm not sitting on a bloody bench!' her husband roared, seeing red. He turned to Gustin and barked: 'Gustin, go to the house and fetch two chairs!'

Gustin lowered his head once more. He took a step forward. How could he go when he was in the next scene, right after the polkist? How?

'Bhatcar . . .'

'Go, Gustin, now! We've been standing a good while now, so be quick about it.'

Gustin retreated without a word, humbly, and ran off into the night.

Just then the band struck up a deafening cacophony and the crowd, as one, roared with laughter. Lithe and jiggly, Paulu the polkist made his entrance. Yet again, as every year, he was about to tell his sorry tale.

Fidelity

'Why don't we stay here tonight?' asked Luísa when she'd finished retouching her lipstick. 'We could send down for something to eat . . . '

Chandracanta didn't reply. He stood by the window, staring out past the curtain at the little square cobblestones in the street.

'I really can't face going back to the boarding house,' she continued. 'It's sad to sleep alone on such a cold night, don't you think?'

He went on looking at the fine rain that came down almost imperceptibly. People hurried by, collars turned up against the weather, not making a sound.

'Chandra!' she exclaimed, turning around. 'Are you listening?'

The young man started, as if waking from a dream, but still didn't answer. He remained where he stood, facing the windowpane. Luísa padded across the room in her bare feet, and hugged him from behind.

'Chandra,' she whispered. 'Have I ever said your name reminds me of baby talk? Chandra! Do you see? Had you never noticed?'

Chandracanta smiled and, taking her arms in his hands, turned himself around. But the expression on his face unsettled Luísa. He seemed sad and burdened, as if very far away.

'Chandra, do you remember the first time we met?' she asked.

He frowned in surprise and raised his head. 'The first time we met?' he repeated.

'Yes. Don't you remember? Of course we'd already seen each other around the Faculty, but that was the first time we were properly introduced. Do you remember?'

Chandracanta gave a slight smile.

'In class . . .'

She laughed out loud.

'That's right. In anatomy class. We talked about where you're from and you told me that story . . .'

'What story?' he wanted to know.

'You're such a scatterbrain! The one about how in Goa you study anatomy with dummies because the students refuse to cut open dead bodies. How funny! Whatever made you think that up?'

Chandracanta pushed her arms away and took a couple of steps forward. Stopping next to the bed, he stood there for a moment, his hands in his pockets and a pensive look on his face. Then he sat down. She remained standing, smiling at him.

'It's true', he said. 'We Orientals have too high a conception of mankind to dare touch cadavers.'

She laughed gleefully.

'Don't tell me you were serious!' she exclaimed.

Chandracanta sighed.

'There're many things you just can't understand. We don't touch corpses, we don't eat meat . . . '

'The sacred cows! Is it really true that you worship cows?'

'In a sense.'

Luísa went over and sat on the edge of the bed by his side. She regarded him for a moment, saying nothing. Then, in silence, she lifted her skirt and began to straighten out her stockings.

'Tell me about your wife', she asked a moment later. 'You say she's fourteen? How odd! You mean you got married and never . . . What's her name?'

'Dhruva!' Chandracanta murmured. 'Dhruva!'

'Dhruva!' she repeated. 'It's a strange name. Like a sort of puffing sound. But I don't find it ugly. Dhruva, Dhruva, Dhruva . . . In time one can even find a certain beauty to it. But fourteen years old! Of course you didn't . . . '

Chandracanta smiled wanly.

Luísa continued to speak: 'Good God! Fourteen! That's not right. She's no more than a child. What does a girl of fourteen know about anything?'

'She knows one thing at least,' muttered Chandracanta.

'Which is?'

'How to go on.'

'To go on?' Luísa asked, frowning and looking him straight in the eye.

'There are many things you just can't understand,' said the young man.

She stretched out a leg, gave her stocking a good tug to flatten it, before piping up once more: 'But fourteen years old! Of course, it's no surprise you're out there . . . A marriage like that has no legitimacy. You didn't even have a wedding night. *Non consummatus*. It's clear-cut, uncomplicated. After it's all been resolved, we can study tropical medicine and then go out to Africa. Wouldn't you like that? We could both make good money. Chandra! Chandra!'

But Chandracanta had his eyes fixed on the curtains and was far, far away from there. In his mind he saw the pure white figure of the priest, the sacred knots of the tali his trembling hands had tied, the invocations to the sacred couples, Shiva and Parvati, Brahma and Sarasvati, Vishnu and Lakshmi, that they bless the newlyweds with their favours. He saw again the infantine figure of Dhruva, his child bride: 'Chand, what's wrong? Chand, are you really going to leave?' And his mother dabbing the kumkum on her forehead, which bound her forever to their family and would give her no choice but to become a bodki . . .

'Chandra!'

Luísa's voice roused him once more, with a hard shake. He looked her square in the face.

'Don't you agree, Chandra? Aren't you listening, Chandra? About going to Africa, Chandra? After you get the divorce sorted out, Chandra?'

Chandracanta stared unwaveringly into her eyes.

'There are many things you just can't understand, Luísa', he repeated. 'Many things . . . You see, this is how we are in the East. The man might stray but the husband is always faithful . . .'

I

Given a choice between the river and the open sea, Bostião would pick the former without hesitation. At dawn each day, he went forth in his canoe, rowing laboriously out to the stakes where he strung his nets. But river fish are measly, and yield little profit. To continue like this, at the mercy of chance, was untenable. Barely covering his daily expenses would no longer do. Life shows no mercy to the weak and nor do our fellow men. It was an old lesson which time imparted pitilessly. As a result, each year, when the mackerel returned, he braved the open sea with the others, despite his age and the great weariness of his body.

'Leave yourself be at home, man. The sea is too much for you now,' his wife would say to him.

It was true. His scrawny body, worn out by over six decades of toil, was growing weak, faltering under the strain. Yet he kept on, screwing up his courage into strength.

'Don't fret, Angelina! You know I'd rather not go. Once there was the lure of adventure . . . but the sea only entices the young. For old-timers like me it holds no attraction.'

After the monsoon, when the large shoals began to appear, this scene would recur each day. And each day it would end in tears and entreaties.

'Don't go, Father . . . . Stay in the river! Prawns fetch money too . . . ' his daughter would plead with all the tenderness of her twenty years, remembering other fishermen who had set out one day never to return.

Bostião tried to explain, every which way he could, his position in Shudra society. The duties he couldn't shirk that enslaved him. He was well aware that in the village all the girls Carminha's age were getting married. Around the neighbourhood, whispered comments passed from mouth to mouth: 'Just when will Bostião marry off his daughter?' they asked, shaking their heads sadly, filled with apprehension. Bostião knew this. Heard this. Felt this. It pained him, but what could he do? He alone knew how hard it was to make ends meet. But one thing was certain. In the words of the other fishermen was a veiled reproach. They expected him to earn enough for his daughter to marry, even though he was old and could barely row out to the stakes each morning to collect his nets. That was just the way things were, and had been since time immemorial, Bostião well knew. And they were right. If girls go past the age . . . and it wouldn't be the first time it happened! 'The body gives poor counsel, arrangements must be made as soon as girls begin to awaken,' they said, with time-honoured wisdom.

'I'll never scrape your dowry together selling prawns,' Bostião muttered. 'Do you think I can die in peace without seeing you settled? It's like a weight inside me, and I feel so old!'

'If only Sapai hadn't fallen ill . . . ' exclaimed his wife, referring to her father-in-law. 'We spent everything we had and more besides! And even then he didn't recover from that damn malaria . . . '

'It wasn't malaria, Angelina! We thought it was, but the doctor said lung trouble all along. If we'd listened to him from the start, perhaps Father could have been saved . . . '

Their house had no clock. They measured time by the rising and setting of the sun, by the opening and closing of the shops, by the arrival and departure of the ferries and, lastly, by the bells of the village church in Penha de França.

After dinner, the family said its prayers. Bostião then went out, lighting a bidi and leaving his wife and daughter to wash the copper plates and earthen vessels.

He crouched in the doorway. It had been cemented over not long previously, before Sapai had fallen ill, when things had been less desperate and they still had some rupees put aside. He gazed out at the river before him, the tranquil, paternal river.

Bostião spent many hours here, smoking in long draws, alone with his thoughts. Sometimes he would just sit and stare, his mind a blank. At others, he would let his thoughts roam free. But they always returned to

Carminha, as they did that day. He thought of her and the little time he had left, how he had grown old. 'Who wants a girl without a dowry?' he thought. 'A girl without a dowry, who'd want her?' he repeated. He stared on, wide-eyed, immobile, until he heard Gustin's voice from the quay.

'Bostião! Hey, Bostião, let's go!'

It was a wrench to leave the comfort of his home, the protection of its palm-leaf roof, the warmth of the stove in which the coals were not quite spent, to pass the whole night at sea, locked in a struggle he no longer wanted any part of. And then, that cold, the wet night air, and the sea wind that left his whole body shivering . . .

Lazily he stretched out his legs, took one more drag on his bidi and rubbed his hands. But before long he heard Vitoba: 'Hey, Bostião, let's go!'

'Just a moment . . . '

'We've got to leave with the tide!'

Bostião sprang to his feet, determination showing through in every movement. Carminha handed him his cambolim with a smile. Bostião slung it round his shoulders and walked off slowly to meet his companions.

Carminha stood and watched in silence. When her father turned back towards her, she smiled again.

More than ever it was necessary to inspire courage in him. Her chances of getting married were at stake. Her future prospects as a woman were in his hands. She often asked herself how long she would remain prey to the sharp eyes of neighbours, family members and local gossips.

What's more, those burning urges she had from time to time, disturbances that left her beside herself, which made her almost shout out loud . . . At heart, however, she was not so greatly troubled. Within Carminha was a natural simplicity that kept her on an even keel. Had her father not spoken with such frankness maybe she would have remained caught up in the whirl of youth and taken far longer to realize the true nature of her predicament. She was happy going to market to sell her father's catch. This trip alone represented a small yet seductive adventure into society. At Mapuçá market she could chat with the young men who came back from Bombay, or further afield, to spend their holidays in Goa. They would brag about sights seen abroad, perhaps exaggerating, she knew, in order to impress the locals. Carminha liked them. They were stylish. They had a different way about them, wore lots of brilliantine in their hair and always came to market in pyjama trousers unlike the fishermen who almost only used a langotim.

In the doorway, eyes closed, Carminha breathed in the fresh breeze from the river. She recalled one by one the young men with brown faces who appeared in the village each year, their glistening hair, the wide horizons in their eyes. And, turning them over in her mind, she fell asleep on the cement floor while old Bostião, stretched to the limit, slogged his guts out at sea.

II

Next morning, very early, the women gathered anxiously on the wharf and peered out towards the mouth of the river. They placed their baskets on the ground and sat down beside them, unfazed by the already scorching sun. On the water the traffic was just getting started. Vessels ferrying people over to their jobs in Pangim crossed to and fro. The women sat and stared, motionless, hoping that the big boat would appear, the big boat with no tarpaulin cover filled with a fine catch.

Suddenly the women broke into smiles. They smiled in unison because it was as if they were one woman. Their hearts leapt in unison, for it was their men who were returning on the big boat which now approached. The women smiled. At their sides stood baskets that would soon be full of silvery mackerel.

'Our men are rowing in silence today. Perhaps they didn't have any luck . . . ' one of them murmured.

'No. Maybe you're wrong. It's the right season!' said another.

'I can't see Bostião among them!' exclaimed a third.

They stopped short, nudging one another in silence until the boat drew in. The men stooped low, lifting Bostião up in their arms.

The women shivered and turned to stare at Angelina. Her eyes widened, the hem of her capodd twisted between her fingers.

Suddenly, from her very guts, she let out a raw cry of anguish and dismay.

'Oh, Deva, Deva, my Bostião! Deva!'

The other women crowded round Angelina, blocking her view, while the men carried Bostião home.

Angelina followed behind, sobbing all the way and wailing: 'Oh, Deva, Deva, look how they've brought me back Bostião!'

When the men arrived, the women moved aside so she could approach her husband who was stretched out on a mat.

'Oh, Bostião!' she cried, sinking to her knees.

But the men had already begun to act.

'Bring some canji,' Salvador ordered, imposing silence.

To bring someone around from a faint, Gustin recommended wafting an onion soused in firewater under their nose.

'Some feni to revive him!'

Carminha was on her way back from the well with two pitchers of water. Seeing the crowd, she shuddered. Oneof the pitchers fell from her head, drenching the cow-dung floor.

'Father!' she sobbed.

'I've already sent for the distican,' someone said. This word alone expressed what they thought had caused Bostião's plight.

Angelina rubbed coconut oil onto her husband's chest and arms with all her might. Little by little, Bostião came to his senses. He opened his eyes and swallowed a little of the canji a neighbour was spooning into his mouth.

'Eat, Bostião, so you get well again!' she said, refusing to take no for an answer.

At that moment the distican arrived, huffing and puffing.

A small woman around fifty years old, she was brisk and full of self-assurance. Her hair, thick with coconut oil, was tied up in a bun. She gave the patient an astute look and wrinkled her nose. Walking around to the far side of the mat, she crouched in front of Bostião and waved her hand across his face. He shut his eyes, exhausted.

'I need salt and three peppers,' the distican shouted hoarsely. Without taking her eyes off the fisherman, she began loudly and rhythmically to pray:

Satmantam
Deva bapa sarvhukumdar . . .

I believe in God,
The Father Almighty . . .

One of the women passed her the peppers and the salt. The old woman leant over and trailed them three times across the ill man's body, repeating:

Satmantam
Deva bapa sarvhukumdar . . .
Sorguincho ani samsaracho rachnar . . .

I believe in God,
The Father Almighty . . .
Creator of Heaven and earth . . .

Afterwards, amid the general silence, she got to her feet and threw the peppers into the fire. A tongue of brighter flame flashed up and a crackling sound was heard.

Angelina turned to the other women: 'See? Didn't I say it was down to the evil eye?'

'It's no surprise!' Florinda chipped in. 'Lately everyone has been saying: "Old Bostião still has what it takes to go mackerel fishing." I knew it then. They should have called in the distican even before he set out to sea!'

'He'll be all better by Wednesday. I guarantee Wednesday's the day to lift the evil eye,' said the old woman, standing in the doorway.

Angelina reached out her hand and gave the woman four tangas, which she shoved into her pocket. Then she turned away satisfied, and set off for home.

As soon as the distican had left, people started to file out of Bostião's shack.

'Send for me if you need anything,' said Tomso.

'If you need any money . . . I'm not rich, but I can scrape something together,' Gustin said quietly.

'Don't cry, Carminha,' said Venctexa, who had come to buy fish and then stayed after learning what had happened. 'Go to my house. My wife will give you a root. Rub it on a stone with some water and then place it on your father's forehead. He'll get better straight away, you'll see. Up and about in no time,' he guaranteed.

III

Bent low, Dr Amoncar was having trouble checking the patient's heartbeat.

'It's always the same story, the same old story!' he grumbled. 'Why didn't you send for me before? First you call the distican, then the gaddi, and then me only as a last resort! How many times have I told you not to take palliatives?'

Gustin, Tomso, Vitoba, Franxavier and Savitri stood at Bostião's feet. Sharp ribs seemed to pierce through his desiccated skin. At the doctor's words, the group bowed their heads, anguish etched on every face.

Dr Amoncar had grown accustomed to expressing himself bluntly. It was part of his routine, a mechanical response. He had become hardened and was under no illusion that the fishermen would obey; this also was true. These people had their distican in whom they had great faith. To take that away would perhaps do more harm than good. To Amoncar what was more urgent was to lift them out of their ignorance, to remove their inner disdain for progress. Admittedly, when all was said and done, this ignorance allowed them a happiness of sorts, yet it was also what left them powerless, subject to each and every misfortune.

'If it's a question of your fee, Doctor . . . '

The doctor interrupted before Gustin could finish his sentence: 'Fee! You know I've never cared a fig about my patients' money, man. I treat the poor without receiving a paisa in return. I'm interested in the way you live your lives, don't you understand?' It pained him to speak harshly once more but he was conscious of fulfilling a duty. His main task was not to treat the patients but to exert his influence over them. He had to enter the minds of these Dravidian fishermen he knew so well and whom, in consequence, he esteemed as the true men they surely were. He knew that they allowed themselves to be governed by instinct, and that their lives were ruled by omens. So he sought, whenever possible, to impart to them the most elementary rules for the treatment of their ills. 'Before them, millions of men lived in ignorance,' he thought. 'These men will learn too one day.' He smiled gently, reflecting on the incalculable progress made by man, that sad yet clever ape.

He finished writing out the prescription, then hesitated before passing it to one of the men.

'You can collect some of these medicines from my house. The others you will have to buy yourselves.'

Vitoba edged meekly forward: 'Thank you, Doctor. Tell us what we have to do to help rid Bostião of this sickness.'

'He can't go on sleeping on the floor. Don't you at least have a mattress?'

'A mattress . . . ? No, Doctor,' Carminha stammered.

By this time Dona Lavínia had come in. She had entered unseen but wasted no time in making herself noticed. She cut in: 'If it's a bed you need, I can lend you one, but without a mattress. It's got boards underneath, all you need do is put a mat on top and it'll be fine.'

The fishermen stared in surprise. Her conscience must have been pricked. Despite frequent 'charity visits', Dona Lavínia was incapable of lending—much less giving—anything to anyone. Confronted with pressing misfortune, she would say: 'May God help you!' and add: 'God knows I struggle to make ends meet.' Everybody knew this to be a lie. Her husband had left her a substantial inheritance, including lands rich in coconuts and rice, and her two sons had found comfortable positions in the Persian Gulf from where they sent home a generous monthly allowance.

Gustin hadn't forgiven Dona Lavínia for refusing to lend him a handful of fine rice when his daughter had taken ill and the doctor had forbidden her to eat corangute. Wanting to teach Dona Lavínia a lesson, he retorted: 'There's no need, Lavin-bai. Poor we may be, but we can always make do for a bed.'

The others pursed their lips in smiles of approval. Angelina took advantage of events to avenge the humiliation she had felt when, during the litany of the Cross, Dona Lavínia had refused to sell her coconuts to make a sweet for her guests. She added ironically: 'We don't want your bed, Lavin-bai. If worse comes to the worst, we can always lay a mat out across a few boards . . . '

'What riffraff!' Dona Lavínia exclaimed in Portuguese to the doctor. 'Miserable ingrates, the lot of them. What arrogance!'

She didn't hide her disdain for the behaviour of the 'common herd'. The only thing that allowed her to save face, and gain a measure of revenge, was the opportunity to flaunt her Portuguese to the 'riffraff' who spoke only Konkani.

This exchange only increased Dr Amoncar's admiration for these humble, dark-skinned Shudras. At heart, he detested this silly little woman who was so tiresome and presumptuous, a consummate hypocrite, a ruthless exploiter of her own mundcars. He replied angrily: 'You're wrong, Dona Lavínia. These people aren't riffraff, and you'd do well not to confuse dignity with arrogance! There are so many things this invalid obviously needs and what do you do? Offer to lend him a bed. Not even give—just lend. What about the rest? Bostião needs more: medicines, injections, a good diet, tonics . . . Where on earth is he going to get the money for all this? For my part, I shan't receive a single paisa for my work and will try to get him his medicine for free.'

Dona Lavínia blushed crimson, before hitting back: 'You defend the dignity of these people, yet forget mine which is of a higher order. Like you, I too am a Brahmin. As for handouts, each of us gives what we can. Our consciences are known only to ourselves and to God, Doctor.'

Dr Amoncar shrugged indifferently. Dona Lavínia grimaced with displeasure and wiped her face with her hand. Rising abruptly from the only chair in the ill-lit room, she mouthed a pretext to rush back home.

'As a good Christian, I had to fulfil my duty to visit the patient,' she said, holding her hand out to the doctor. 'But I cannot stay, you must understand. My sons arrived back from the Gulf yesterday, and the preparations for their welcome reception are not yet complete, you must understand . . . '

She felt much better on the way home. 'What riffraff!' she grumbled, regretting ever having gone there. 'Heaped up like ants in that wretched little room, with that slit of a window that hardly lets in any air. Phew! How close it was!'

No sooner had she arrived home than she flopped down in her *cadeira voltaire* and began to cool herself nervously with a fan bought at the fair of Our Lady of the Immaculate Conception. This gesture signalled that she was not in a good mood.

Entering the room, her eldest son Robin asked: 'Mama, are you feeling poorly?'

'I'm fine,' Dona Lavínia snapped. 'It's just that those people in the village are getting airs above their station. I've just been to that fisherman Bostião's house and those riffraff really got my goat. The worst of it was that doctor. He's in cahoots with them all.'

Robin spotted a chance to impress his mother with the knowledge he'd acquired in far-off lands: 'That doctor is probably a communist!'

'Heavens above!' murmured Dona Lavínia. 'These newfangled terms are too much for me . . . what was that again?'

IV

At Bostião's a veritable battle was being waged between the fishermen and the doctor. Dr Amoncar was striving to explain that the patient had tuberculosis and needed to be admitted to the sanatorium. Nobody would listen.

'No, Doctor, I won't go to hospital! Leave me be here with my people! I'd prefer to die in my own village, in my own house, surrounded by Gustin, Vitoba, Tomso and my neighbours. No, doctor, no hospital! Never!'

The patient's feeble words were drowned out by Angelina's shrill voice: 'Dr Amoncar, if you don't want to treat my husband just be upfront about it. We'll call in another doctor. If we must we'll even pawn our fishing nets and copperware!'

'You can count on me, Angelina,' chipped in Gustin, 'I'm not rich, but I can always find some money for Bostião somewhere!'

'You can count on me too!' added Vitoba. 'Chin up, Carminha. Your father'll not leave this house!'

Dr Amoncar was on the verge of giving in. He found himself on a strange battlefield, where feelings and traditions outfought reason and where he had no hope of triumph. He decided to switch tack. He turned to the patient and said with great sincerity: 'Look Bostião, forget that I'm a doctor. Let's talk man-to-man, OK? Tell me something, do you remember how it was your father died?'

'Yes, sir, it wasn't malaria . . . It was lung trouble . . . ' He turned over onto his side to face the doctor, making the boards of the improvised bed groan in the process. 'You wanted him to go into hospital too. I remember it well, Dr Amoncar.'

'Now listen to me: you've got your father's condition. Do you get that? You need to be admitted to hospital. If you don't go, it'll be bad for you and bad for the others—they could catch your illness. If you do go, you'll get better and be home in no time!'

Bostião stopped and stared, thinking it over. He looked the doctor straight in the eye, trying to work out whether he was telling the truth, and then nodded, finally convinced. Dr Amoncar was an honest man, and never misled anybody. He'd said the same thing about Sapai and nobody had wanted to listen. And Sapai had died. Dr Amoncar was right: Sapai had died because he hadn't gone to hospital. He looked at the doctor, his mind made up: 'The others can catch my illness, Doctor? I'll go then . . . I don't want to be anyone's ruin. I'll go to your hospital . . .'

On their Dravidian faces a mixture of guilt and admiration signalled the dignified acceptance of defeat. As for Dr Amoncar, he could consider himself the victor. Yet instead of triumph, all he felt was pain. There was a lump in his throat, and he found it hard to speak.

At that moment, and against her own wishes, Dona Lavínia entered the room which reeked of medicaments and incense. She'd decided never again to cross that threshold but her damn conscience had rounded on her and wouldn't leave her alone. She had gone to confession to regain some peace of mind, and the priest had ordered that she humble herself in penitence: 'Go back to Bostião's and take him succour. You have no right to curse or despise those people. They are Shudras. You inherited your wealth and caste from your forbears, and thus have done nothing to deserve either. Remember the words of God: *It is easier for a camel to pass through the eye of a needle, than for a rich man to enter the Kingdom of Heaven.*' So she had no choice but to go. She went unwillingly, however. One couldn't go soft on these people, or they would take advantage. Looking fixedly at Bostião she walked to the centre of the room. And then, slowly, so that everyone could see her generosity, she took a rupee from her bag and placed it in the patient's hand.

'This is for milk!' she said, stressing the word 'milk' which those people never drank. 'God speed your recovery. I shall pray for you,' she added and was instantly moved by her own piety.

'Thank you, Lavin-bai,' Angelina murmured. 'Pray also for Carminha, who now needs her father more than ever, and for all the fisherfolk of Orlim.'

In his head, Dr Amoncar calculated the time it would take to transfer the patient to hospital. He couldn't let another night pass, for fear they might change their minds.

'Right, you'd better get a boat ready to transport Bostião,' he exclaimed. 'I've already spoken to the hospital. All you have to do is show them this letter.'

He took a letter from his coat pocket and handed it to Gustin, the head of the group.

'Don't forget to show this at the hospital. The rest is already taken care of.'

Venctexa made a sign for the others to follow him out. Only Gustin stayed behind, listening attentively to the doctor's instructions.

'Let's see if our boat's got stuck in the soft mud. The tide's on its way out.'

The next moment, the distican appeared. She'd run all the way from the market where she'd heard the news, and was exhausted. She squeezed her way past the women and offered her help, only there was nothing left to do. Angelina had made up a little bundle of clothes and was now crying, wiping away her tears with the hem of her capodd. When the fishermen returned, their feet dark with mud, her sobbing increased until it became an animal-like keening.

'What are you waiting for? You'd better take him . . . ' Dr Amoncar growled in a harsh voice that was not his own.

Angelina, Carminha, Savitri and Dona Lavínia wept as if there, before such pain, they were equal, no longer divided by caste until their dying day.

Bostião glanced up one final time at his old village: his house with its palm-leaf roof, his wife and daughter, the friends who until the last hadn't abandoned him. In the distance, the Church of Our Lady of Penha de França, mirrored in the Mandovi, rose up like a beacon of hope.

On the wharf, nothing but the sound of oars against water. And Carminha, frozen, like a statue of resignation.

Memory of Tio Salu

You could say that everything I carry inside forms a temple of saudade. Around me now, in a painful gyre, now swirls my entire childhood in that old village by the Mandovi. Back then time seemed to stand still and we lived as we did a thousand years ago, as we always had.

Even today, when I shut my eyes, I see the dark-skinned fishermen, slender yet robust, as they set out in their narrow boats each morning. As they did back then. As they always had. I still hear them as they sit on the wooden pier behind their shacks and talk about the weather, their work, the sea, neighbourhood gossip, life . . . To this day nostalgia speaks to me in their guttural voices.

Every afternoon, as I stepped off the *gasolina* from Pangim, there was always a smiling face to ask: '*Aiz Ponge, baiee*?'—So you went to Pangim today, miss?

Or when, in the verandah overlooking the river, as night fell and they walked hurriedly by, their nets slung over their shoulders: '*Dista tyepramanem ho varo pavsala, baiee*!—This wind'll bring rain, miss!

A good village it was, full of good people, good mundcars, fishermen, Curumbins, Farazes, old men and women, Catholics and Hindus and the little boys in dirty loincloths I played hopscotch or goddé with so often, boys with lively little brown faces who gave me delicious tamarind chinchré to nibble on at school.

How we would sing back then, all equal, before the hands of adults dug a gulf between us, siblings in our larks and inconsequential hopes, the future mundcars and bhatcars:

Undir mojea mama
Anim aum sangtam tuca
Tum mazrichea pilea
Laguim khellu mandunaca . . .

My Uncle Mouse
There's something I want to say
With the cat's son
Don't you go off and play.

And then, suddenly, off we would shoot, giving gleeful cries of: 'Here comes Tio Salu!'

Tio Salu . . .

I shall never forget that Christmas. So sad, so distant now it hardly seems real. It's as if I can see everything before me once more, the bright, festive village, the freshly white-washed houses adorned with Chinese lanterns, cones and bamboo stars . . . Every Christmas was exactly the same yet always so different! The air would be heavy with scents. In the kitchens, plump oddé fried in oil, a thousand tasty sweets, and in the front room the whole family would gather to arrange the Nativity scene, placing little figures made of wood or cardboard amid the green blades of nachni.

That Christmas, my mother decided to invite over tio Salu who lived alone on the other side of the village. I clapped my hands with joy. Unable to contain myself, I skipped off down the road to fetch him.

'Tio Salu, tio Salu, come and spend Christmas with us!'

He stroked my hair pensively.

'Today I won't leave my house!' he answered in an almost pained voice.

Then, when he saw my sad, disappointed expression, he gave a faint smile.

'Come with me!' he said, taking my hand. 'Let me show you something . . . '

In the corner of the room stood his Nativity scene. It lacked for nothing, not even a faded cut-out of the Three Wise Kings.

'It's marvellous!' I exclaimed, my child's eyes filled with wonder.

But already tio Salu was dragging me towards the kitchen to see the sweets.

'All sent over by people from the village. They know I'm too old to make my own dinner on Christmas Eve . . . They haven't forgotten me!'

But something was missing. He gestured for me to follow and walked out into the garden. There, on a wooden pole in the ground hung a bamboo star. Its green paper lining was shabby and discoloured. But it was a star, a huge star, and I wanted to offer my congratulations.

'Tio Salu . . . ' I turned around.

He was crying. The distressed expression on his wrinkled face made it look all the more crumpled.

'Tio Salu . . . tio Salu . . . ' I exclaimed, not knowing what to do.

The old man just stood there, eyes fixed on the star. Then he strode across and sat down on a mound of loose stones nearby.

'My little one, baiee, please forgive me. When you get to my age, when you've left everything and everyone behind, the slightest thing can set you off . . . You cry at the drop of a hat. When all's said and done, I'm no more than a poor abandoned old man . . . '

My voice caught in my throat and I was barely able to stammer a reply: 'No. That's not true. You're loved and respected. Everyone remembers you at Christmas!'

Tio Salu fingered a dhumti and said nothing. He raised it to his mouth, lit the end and began to smoke, mumbling all the while. I couldn't understand. I didn't know what he was saying. It was a jumbled murmur that seemed to go on forever.

I took a step forward, my mind made up: 'They must be waiting for us. Let's go!' I said, trying to inject some enthusiasm into my voice.

Tio Salu got his rosary out instinctively, and when he saw that I hadn't moved, whispered: 'I'm going to pray, baiee, that you and your family have a merry Christmas. This might be my last, so I want to spend it in my own house . . . '

I kissed his hand and returned home with a heavy heart, a sadness I wasn't quite able to fathom.

The next day, after lunch, someone came and announced: 'Poor old Salu is dead! This year he didn't even change the lining on his star. Maybe he knew his time was up . . .'

At that very moment a group of Farazes walked past, and in loud voices intoned: *'Noman Morie, curpen bolele . . .'* —Hail Mary, full of grace . . .

All this is engraved on my soul, every single little thing, like some heavy ballast that I cannot remove nor wish to. Even today, I close my eyes on occasion and see my old village, the fishermen, the tranquil waters of the Mandovi, and I repeat under my breath: *'Noman Morie, curpen bolele . . .* ', a prayer that my homeland, my countrymen and the language of my forebears never wither away inside me.

The Cure

Rosu looked around and saw that she was alone. Her companions had gone. They must have scattered out across the hill.

The monsoon was almost upon them. Within weeks it would pour down on the parched land in a deluge. And then would come long monotonous days, when the rain drummed against the palm-leaf roofs and the meadows flooded. Everything on land would be drenched, fields and homes, trees and men. Reserves of firewood were needed, so everyone came to stock up. Each afternoon, the women of the village went out to the hill, returning home at dusk, their bodies swaying as they carried great bundles of wood on their heads, which they would then stack in small huts protected by olas.

Rosu looked around, unsettled by the silence that. surrounded her. The light was growing dim, taking on a greyish tone. Soon the hill would be transformed into a huge eerie black mound. Rosu hesitated. She couldn't leave behind the wood she'd gathered with such effort. But how could she carry such a heavy load back to the village?

Despite herself she began to imagine terrible things. Standing there alone, she pictured snakes and spirits and felt herself break out in a cold sweat. She recalled the stories the elders of the village would tell, of vengeful snakes and spirits that dragged people down to hell. It was said that by night the ghost of Zogu roamed these parts. That Kristna had gone mad one night when she had come out to the hill alone. Rosu had never met the girl but her mother had, and whenever Kristna's name was mentioned, she'd see the faces round her darken with sorrow. She felt a shiver run through her body. And here she was alone. And the ghost of Zogu . . . and the vengeful snakes . . . Gripped by uncontrollable terror, Rosu dropped her firewood and bolted down the hill. Almost immediately, scared senseless, hardly having gone two steps, she tripped and fell. She hadn't had a second to pull herself together and calm her pounding heart when she heard footsteps hurrying in her direction.

'Don't be scared!' said Caxinata in a cheery voice as he drew near.

'Oh!' sighed Rosu with relief. 'It's good to see a familiar face . . . I've no idea where Gebel, Romusa and Savitri have got to!'

And on she chattered, to hear her own voice aloud and soothe her fright. Caxinata's appearance had calmed her down. Everyone knew Caxinata. He was just the man for such a situation. It was well known in the village that Caxinata was utterly fearless. He was the bravest fellow in the neighbourhood, famed for his valour in killing snakes or confronting evil spirits. And he was obliging, ever ready to lend a hand. If anybody needed a doctor or a priest, there was Caxinata, always ready to hare off into the distance to fetch one. If an invalid had urgent need of medicine or some ice, who else but Caxinata to hie down to the city, even if that meant making his way across hills and cemeteries at all hours of the night? Safe in the knowledge that she was not alone, Rosu sighed with relief. Now she had no cause for worry. No longer did she have to abandon her precious firewood and dash for home.

For Caxinata this meeting was one of the happiest moments in his life. He had been coming out to the hill for some time now, to linger in the hope of talking to Rosu far from the prying eyes of other villagers. But whenever Rosu showed up, she was in company. On that day, as the other women dispersed after calling out her name several times, he'd hidden behind a cashew tree and watched as Rosu grew increasingly frightened. He understood the source of her indecision and was readying himself to emerge like a guardian angel when, against all expectation, Rosu had upped and fled. Caxinata dithered, unsure whether to run after her but then decided that to do so risked a misunderstanding. At that moment he raised his eyes to heaven and hoped desperately for something to intervene, something that might hold her back . . . When he saw her stumble on the rocks, he took fright, and regretted having been, albeit in thought alone, the cause of her fall . . .

On the other hand, that fall was providential, since it meant he no longer had to hide behind the cashew. He could do what any other man in his position would. Confident that not a glimmer of his hidden purpose was apparent, he walked straight up to Rosu. She had given him the chance to approach and perhaps give expression to his desires. This wasn't just some impulse, something vague and indistinct, but the certainty of a long-cherished dream, treasured deep within, far from the barrier separating Hindus and Catholics. There, on that very hillside, surrounded only by the sky and the trees, without witnesses, he could share his love, this forbidden love that must remain forever secret on pain of their ruthless expulsion from the society of their fellows.

They walked slowly on, linked by the odd feeling of not being alone. Caxinata carried Rosu's bundle of firewood on his head. She held him back by the arm when a rock appeared in his path and kept watch to ensure his shirt didn't snag on the thorns of the karonda bushes.

'Are you still scared?' Caxinata asked suddenly, without stopping.

'No!' Rosu answered. 'How could I be when you're the bravest man in Orlim?'

But her reply didn't satisfy Caxinata. He wanted to hear more from those evasive lips. He tried again, this time directly.

'And aren't you scared of me? If we were in the village, you wouldn't be seen in my company, I know . . . '

'You don't understand . . . you see . . . I . . . ' she murmured, fumbling for an excuse. But what did she need an excuse for, if they'd been in the village she would have just retorted rudely or even insulted him. The indulgent way in which she spoke to this Hindu, of whom nothing could be expected, surprised her. Truth be told, she was little inclined to speak to men; only with Bentu, Ladru, Tomso and the other boys from the neighbourhood she always found a way to exchange a little banter. Hindus, however, she shunned whenever she could. For this reason, her answer went unfinished. She smiled and bowed her head.

'You don't have to reply. I understand . . . ' Caxinata whispered.

As they approached the village, the first houses began to appear amid trees, dominated by the whitewashed stone of Bhatcar Dias' mansion. Caxinata noticed Rosu start to show signs of impatience, to cough and regain her usual, slightly haughty, air which stood in clear contrast to the gentle words she'd spoken on the way. But deep in her heart, and without knowing why, Rosu was reluctant to part from Caxinata. Despite this feeling, despite her desire to be tactful, still she couldn't hide her fear that someone might spot them together. The little grocer's shops, lit up by Petromax lamps, lent life to the village. At that hour, the men would meet there to smoke bidis, drink feni and hold forth on the events of the day. Their wives would be at home, grinding spices or putting the finishing touches to that night's curry. The few women in the streets at night were the occasional fishwives returning late from Mapuçá market. From a far-off gramophone, the voice of an Indian singer reached them, a voice as fine and melodious as a magical lament.

They walked on through the dark, in silence. On the outskirts of the village, by the first mud houses, they stopped. It was time to go their separate ways. Both understood this without need of words.

'If you come to the hill tomorrow, I'll be there, behind the high wall. I go there every day to cut wood for Xamba. I can give you the thin branches. Xamba'll never check . . .'

'Yes . . . tomorrow . . . ' Rosu agreed demurely as Caxinata handed back her bundle.

The next day, setting out before her usual companions, Rosu made her way alone to the hill. She was nervous but also optimistic. Rosu couldn't understand it. All night she had thought she wouldn't go, had made up her mind not to go, but when the moment came she couldn't resist. She walked over mechanically, her mind turned to other things: the arrival of Lavin-bai's children, the terrible illness afflicting Bostião who had been taken to hospital. But on reaching the pile of stones where she and Caxinata had agreed to meet she began to tremble. He must be close by. She could hear the blows of his axe thudding against a tree. Her body shook as she clambered over the wall, and a host of ideas flashed through her mind. Though her conscience ordered her to retreat, something inside drove her on. Perhaps it was the clandestine flavour of that meeting, for the law of her birth didn't allow her to take a Hindu for a husband.

On the other side, seeing her appear, Caxinata dropped his axe and hurried over to help her down, then clasped her tightly in his arms. She didn't resist. Instead she leant against his chest, hunched up and defenceless. Around them were only sky and trees and snake nests. They felt a sudden sense of freedom, something they'd never felt before.

Yet this new emotion alarmed Rosu and left her ill at ease. To dispel these feelings she began, with skittish movements, to gather firewood. She regretted coming. 'But what do I have to be regretful about?' she asked herself.

'Not now,' Caxinata whispered, holding her back. 'Let's talk . . . '

They sat in the shade of a tree and began to sip some cashew juice. The branches above split the sky into a patchwork of blue. Here and there ripe fruit fell onto dry leaves. For a long while they were silent, until Rosu exclaimed: 'What time is it? Gebel and Savitri will be arriving any minute. I have to go and meet them . . . '

Together they looked up at the sun: it must be about three o'clock. She quickly got to her feet and straightened out her clothes and hair. Around her toned neck hung a gold chain adorned with medals of Our Lady and the saints she revered. On her wrists jangled bracelets of glass and silver. Taking her by the arms, Caxinata stared into her eyes.

'I'll only let you go if you promise to come back tomorrow, and the days after, while I'm out here working,' he said forcefully, before trailing off. He spoke again, this time more hesitantly: 'Rosu, for the past weeks I've wanted to ask you something . . . '

'Ask me something? Saiba! Ask what?'

'Nothing, Rosu. Nothing at all. Perhaps we could be happy? If anything happens, the distican can give you a cure . . . '

'A cure, again! Love between a Catholic and a Hindu always ends with a cure. Why can't it be different, legal, without shame or cures?' Rosu pressed herself against Caxinata's chest and began to sob.

'I know,' he murmured. 'I feel the same way. I didn't mean to offend you. It's just the way things have always been, and the way I think they will always be. If it were up to me I'd marry you, Rosu . . . but what do my wishes matter?'

Rosu stepped back from Caxinata, and slowly began to walk away. He didn't try to follow her.

'Do you promise to come back?' he asked simply, in a low voice.

'Yes, tomorrow. After lunch!' she replied, a childish smile lighting up her face once more.

The Supplement

Eucaristino arrived home late that day. His department shut at five and it was already past seven when, at last, he strode in, ramrod straight, full of vigour and with a new gleam in his eyes. The solemn expression he wore unsettled his whole family. Dona Camila stopped and stared in alarm, unsure what to make of him. Yes, because Senhor Eucaristino, an administrative assistant to the Treasury, was normally such a smiling, good-humoured man, adored by his loved ones and so esteemed by his colleagues that he even had a few Hindu friends, something quite rare for descendentes.

However that day, as well as being extraordinarily late, he came in looking absolutely browned off. Such a thing was unheard of, for Senhor Eucaristino was a good family man, reliable and caring. Dona Camila had been hopping mad with him for the past two hours, shuttling back and forth between the altar room and the door. She had even sent Vasquinho down to the Café Moderno to see if his father was there with his colleagues, sipping beer or eating bajipuri. But the little fellow came back out of breath and empty-handed. He'd also asked Senhor Emérico at the post office, yet no one had seen his father. Well, maybe that wasn't quite the case but, as usual, Senhor Emérico was already a few sheets to the wind.

For all these reasons Dona Camila was agog when her husband marched in looking so odd. If Senhor Eucaristino had entered as usual, all smiles and bonhomie, they would have quarrelled for sure, but that expression on his face left his wife speechless.

Eucaristino came in and closed the door with a fierce kick. Before the startled faces of Dona Camila, Vasquinho and Xavierinho, he placed a large package on the table and looked around him, inspecting the room with a fiery look.

'This just won't do!' were his first, decisive words which left his family dumbstruck.

Solemnly he took two steps forwards and stretched out his arms in a broad attitude of despair. He repeated in a melodramatic tone: 'This just won't do!'

By then Dona Camila and the boys could bear the tension no longer: 'Tininho!' she shrieked.

'Paizinho,' the boys chorused.

But Senhor Eucaristino imposed order with a bark.

'Quiet!'

And they all fell silent.

For a few moments only the buzz of flies circling the room could be heard.

Stony-faced, Eucaristino wheeled around, losing his balance as he did and clutching the back of a chair so as not to fall.

Without losing his composure, he said: 'All this must change, change completely!' He gestured broadly around him. 'Have you seen our house, Camila? Throw that tambio away immediately. I don't want junk like that in here anymore, aahn!' He strode out to the kitchen, where he snatched up a doulo and brandished it menacingly. 'I'm going to buy an aluminium ladle, like civilized people have. Give these doulé to the Bonguis. I don't want these things in my home!'

Senhor Eucaristino appeared to have lost his mind. Dona Camila—the boys shielded by her vast bulk—took refuge in a corner. She followed her husband with her eyes, too afraid to open her mouth.

'Now, look here,' the head of the household trumpeted. 'Look at this horrible kitchen. All black, all covered in soot. No more wood fires. They're only fit for Goans. We're going to buy a gas stove, let me tell you. All this is going to change. We're civilized now, we're not like those Goans, aahn! You know that, don't you Camila? We have to live up to our position, so there's no confusion. From now on, no more damn curry. We can't eat food like that. We'll eat salt cod. Bacalhau from now on. Bacalhau and nothing but!

By now Dona Camila could stand it no longer. It was all too much. He'd struck a raw nerve. She cried: 'You're out of your mind, Tininho! How do you want us to eat bacalhau on 200 rupees a month? It's not even enough for curry . . . !'

Eucaristino fell silent for a moment. He wavered, as if overcome by the intransigence of reality. But then he rallied, dismissing any doubts and shutting himself up in his own way of thinking. Of course, in order to do so he had to speak all the louder. So he was practically screaming when he said: 'But we're no longer Goans! We can't let things slip!'

'But Tininho, what about that fish curry you love so much?'

Tininho feigned indifference. 'We have to keep our end up, I tell you. No more apas. You'll buy bread instead of chapatis, Camila. And no more tea. Just coffee. Coffee's the thing. From now on, we'll make no more tea in this house. Always drinking tea! You realize, Milinha, that it's coffee we should drink, not endless cups of tea . . . '

'How on earth shall we do that on 200 rupees a month?' Dona Camila ventured again, in a thin, tattered voice. 'Eh, you must have gone soft in the head, Tininho!'

Suddenly Eucaristino flopped down in his *cadeira voltaire* which reclined with the heavy groan of old wood. For the first time since he arrived, he looked his wife straight in the eye: 'I'm not crazy, Milinha,' he whispered. 'On the contrary, today I feel fine. There's something you don't know . . . !'

He sprang to his feet and stood stiff-legged, an inspired look lighting up his face.

'We're Europeans now, Milinha. We're now Europeans! It's not like it was before!'

'Us, Europeans? Since when are we Europeans?' his wife asked meekly, unwilling to believe him.

'Yes, Milinha, it's true. We're Europeans. They've extended the colonial supplement to descendentes. We're considered European. We're not Goan any more. And we have to keep up appearances, is that clear? Careful with the boys now. Xavierinho! Vasquinho! Come here! Did you know we were Europeans? If you didn't, you do now. Tell your friends. From today on, all descendentes are considered European and receive a supplement. Now we'll eat nothing but bacalhau every day . . . '

Xavierinho pulled a face.

'Chii, codfish! I don't like it, Father . . . if to be European you have to eat bacalhau, I'd rather be Goan . . . '

Eucaristino goggled. He turned to his wife and said: 'Have you heard these children? What cheek, Camila . . . '

'Well, to be honest, Tininho,' she replied, 'I only really like it in fishcakes, those fofos de bacalhau!'

The trials of Eucaristino, dedicated paterfamilias and honest administrative assistant to the Treasury, had now come to a head. With grim resolve, he strode to the package on the table and untied the string. He seized one of the rolls of paper it contained and held it aloft.

'Have you ever seen one of these? Take a good look. It's toilet paper, aahn! All Europeans use toilet paper. No more washing by hand in this house or my name's not Eucaristino da Sagrada Família Mascarenhas de Castro e Bragança . . . '

The Arms of Venus

The monsoon broke furiously. Heavy rains soaked the thin walls of the houses, reducing them to mud, to drowned earth and dung. Gusty winds upset trees and blew tiles from the rooftops. In desperation, the people of the village scurried back and forth, searching for replacement olas to plug the breaches.

The flooded paddies were a desolate sight. Bare-chested Curumbins stood waist deep, scraping out runnels so the brown water could drain muddily away into the river. Loyal to the land, they strived to rescue the seeds, their only food source for the coming year.

From a narrow path on the far side, Bhatcar Dias oversaw their efforts. Wearing only his pyjamas and sandals, sheltering under a vast umbrella, he had come in person to watch as the catastrophe played itself out. He could hardly believe his eyes. To and fro he paced, gesticulating, expressing himself in a language of despair. Tears ran down his face as he envisaged the poor harvest, the famine and misery soon to engulf them. How could such misfortune be explained? He recalled the masses said for the souls of his forbears and in praise of Our Lady of Perpetual Succour. Had something been forgotten? Only if the parish priest, to whom money for the masses had been given in good time, had been remiss. Dias recalled attending every service except that given for the soul of his grandfather. There was the explanation. 'Perhaps it's his revenge!' Relieved by his discovery, he swore to order another mass—a sung one this time—for the soul of the venerable old man from whom he'd inherited his estate.

The face of Bhatcar Dias and the Dravidian features of the Curumbins brightened as clear sky burst through the dark clouds. In the distance, rising from the hills, a vivid rainbow interrupted the monotony of the paddy fields. The downpour would soon be over.

'A rainbow! The weather's clearing! But don't you dare move until all that water's drained away!' the bhatcar roared in the stentorian voice he used when addressing his mundcars.

Saying nothing, they carried on obediently and humbly with their task, their drenched bodies shivering with cold. From time to time the mundcars wrung out their sopping langotins. The women, in palm-leaf hoods, crouched beside their menfolk. Together they tamed the waters. The slackening rain spared only Dias who huddled in his pyjamas under the umbrella.

No one could recall such a deluge in recent years. Whenever the monsoon came late, they would pray for abundant rain so that the seeds, planted with the sweat of their labour, might sprout quickly. This time, however, they implored God for the opposite. For days they'd begged for the rain to cease and the sun—the sun that scorched their backs—to emerge. Now they pleaded for it to save their paddies.

Only the bhatcar's head was raised. His gestures betrayed his intransigence. To intimidate them, he shouted: 'I don't care how you do it, but save those seeds! If the harvest is poor, don't count on me! This year rice is going to be expensive and I'll not give up my share!'

'But, bhatecara, you might lend us some paddy . . . ' Mogrem's voice was tinged with the fear of refusal.

The bhatcar was unmoved. He had anticipated their yearly lament of 'We don't have enough paddy!' Just when he was banking on a good price for the crop! His conscience ordered mercy for the mundcars but Dias was unwilling to give in. Giving in, for him, meant forgoing a tidy profit from the high market prices. He needed to quash Mogrém's hopes straight away. If he lent to her, he'd have to lend to all and would only have enough paddy left for his own household.

'Lend you paddy? No matter how the harvest turns out, you always rely on loans! What about last year's debt?' he grumbled, closing his umbrella and stabbing it into the ground. 'First see if you can settle last year's debt!'

In those words, Mogrém glimpsed the future misery of her home. She was wet through and through. Her blouse had shrunk, leaving her breasts unconstrained. Though profoundly dejected, she did not break faith with her own exuberant beauty. In her grace, in all the melody of her expression, she was still a typical woman of her caste. She swayed gently, her semi-naked husband by her side. Both were appalled by the prospect of such a bad year.

It came as no surprise to see Mogrém and Vitol so downcast. They must have felt battered by fate now that life had become a struggle against hunger. Even their arduous work wasn't enough to feed their children whose bellies were swollen from the rice gruel they ate each day.

First thing in the morning, Mogrém would prepare a huge pot of canji, part of which was for the breakfast and lunch of her children; the rest was for her and Vitol to eat out at the fields. During the day, little Xanta, the eldest daughter, was left in charge of the house. It was she who looked after her five little siblings who roamed around all day. They had lost the habit of crying, even if they needed something or felt unwell. There was no point. They knew no one would come. Xanta, only eight years old, was barely able to maintain order and keep the flock of children safe until their parents' return.

The solidarity of that family touched me deeply. And the poverty that haunted it didn't escape my notice. I went so far as to ask Mogrém indiscreet questions: Why did they bring so many children into the world knowing they hadn't the means to support them?

'Our children are the blessing of our home. In a few years' time, there'll be twelve arms working alongside Vitol and me,' she answered calmly. And her whole body seemed to smile at this vision of the future. To me it just seemed there'd be another twelve arms working for the bhatcar. All the same, Mogrém's outlook was not unfounded.

Compared to his wife, Vitol had aged considerably. His deep premature wrinkles were the mark of an arid life devoid of prospects. All his virility was concentrated in his arms which were scaly and bulging with muscle, over-developed compared to the rest of his body. He carried hidden within him a cloud of fear which revealed itself, however, on days of misfortune.

Good cheer returned as the weather picked up. The rains grew scant or, to be more accurate, just enough rain fell to irrigate the fields. The houses, patched up with olas and bamboo, took on a steadfast appearance. No one gave any more thought to the catastrophic start to that monsoon.

The Curumbins of Orlim returned to work with redoubled purpose. No longer did they fear a difficult, hungry year. Their conversations were filled with the hope the crop would be sufficient; they reassured one another that they would be given their fair share of paddy. They seemed to have no concern but paddy, the central reason for their existence.

In Mogrém's home there was neither hope nor courage, only Vitol trudging out to the fields, dogged by the cloud of fear that cut him off from everyone else. The children no longer played as they had until recently. Their mother's illness must have left them feeling paralysed. She, Mogrém, took palliatives brought from the most distant villages yet her condition worsened by the day. No one called the doctor. The poor tend to place their faith in Mother Nature who determines their joys and sorrows. They merely hoped that the evil spirits would disappear. They had prayed long and hard to that end.

Exhausted by fever, Mogrém eventually died, in the silence that had surrounded her since the opening day of the monsoon. My first thought upon receiving those sad tidings was that Orlim would now be deprived of her Venus-like figure. What a shame I'd never captured her sweet expression on canvas, the elegant melody of her body. Mogrém the beautiful, the beautiful Mogrém had vanished, never knowing her own beauty, a freedom from affectation that had perhaps given me the exact measure of her true grace. It pained me deeply to think of Mogrém dead, ravaged by illness, with nothing to attest her former state. I knew that soon she would be tied to the bamboo stretcher the men were preparing. Soon, too, she would be borne to the crematorium. Before long she would be nothing more than a wisp of smoke.

Tears welled up in Vitol's sunken eyes and trickled down to mix with the sweat on his bare chest. Of their six children, only Xanta wept. Her crying tore at my heart. Her siblings seemed terribly frightened, their eyes blinking in shock. Bhatcar Dias was present too, mute and despondent. His face harboured something that, at that moment, reduced him to Vitol's level. How strange it was to see them so interlinked in attitude, an attitude, it seemed to me, that consisted more of fear than anything else.

For my part, the only thing that mattered was the beauty of the woman whose sparkle death had stolen.

'Mogrém was gorgeous. The most beautiful Curumbina in all Orlim!'

With these words, I hoped to touch Vitol's pain. He remained silent at first and didn't react. But he couldn't hold back for long: 'No, it's not Mogrém's beauty I miss, baiee . . . ' he said, as though confessing. 'Mogrém, for me, meant two strong arms, my best allies in this struggle against hunger!'

Vitol's frank confession, so unlike the weasel words of a bourgeois in such circumstances, met with the bhatcar's full understanding. He nodded in agreement. Now the inner anxiety of the former had been revealed, the attitude of the latter needed no explanation. The fear they showed, which united them at that moment, was not of death or of the woman who now lay lifeless forever: what they feared was the lack of Mogrém's arms! Nothing but her arms, which symbolized toil. Bread for the mundcar as for the bhatcar.

Instinctively I lowered my gaze to Mogrém's arms. But it was too late. Her beauty now lay hidden beneath a shroud. Outside, by the entrance to her home, the men waited to bear her corpse up the hill.

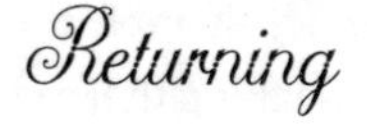

Returning

Dhruva set the plates on the floor and turned to call her husband's grandfather who was lounging in a corner of the house. Crouched with his back against the wall and smoking a bidi, the old man struggled briefly to overcome the cramps that hindered his movements. But as soon as he'd stretched out his muscles and got to his feet, his mood brightened as he looked around.

'Hey Chandracanta, hey Sadassiva, let's eat!' said the old man in a loud voice as he waited for his son and grandson to join him.

Chandracanta seemed not to have heard, and didn't move from his spot before the little iron-barred window. It all seemed so strange to him, this horrible new experience of seeing his memories transformed into out-of-date concepts with which he felt no connection. His home, so snug six years earlier, seemed now like a dead end; his parents, an elderly couple who clung to the land, and all too tightly; his grandfather, a rocky outcrop in which ancestral ideas had struck roots that snaked inalterably through the generations! But the worst thing, the thing that saddened him most, was the lack of communication with Dhruva whose image he had nursed for all those years. Dhruva was no longer the flame that had driven him on but merely a robot plodding around her parents-in-law. How absurd, he thought (despite six years of separation? Or precisely because of it?), that they hadn't yet exchanged more than a few trite comments . . .

'Hey, Chandracanta! Have you washed your hands? Apai and Dada are already eating!' shouted his mother from the far end of the kitchen.

His first impulse was to disobey and stay put. He saw, however, that Dhruva was waiting with the water jug. He walked across to her and stretched his hands out over the sink. Dhruva tipped the jug and let the contents trickle down over the fingers of her husband who, meanwhile, couldn't take his eyes from her face. Without doubt she too felt how odd things were between them. They remained in silence for a few moments and, perhaps for that reason, Dhruva hurried away, covering her face with the hem of her sari as thick tears began to roll down her cheeks.

Chandracanta heaved a deep sigh. He paused for a moment, but his father and his grandfather were waiting for him. In his European-style suit, brought home from Lisbon, he was reluctant to sit down beside them on the floor. He hesitated. But then had an idea: he took the handkerchief from his pocket, laid it out on the floor and then made to sit cross-legged beside them.

'What's that handkerchief for? Is that the way they eat in Portugal?' asked his grandfather, always on the alert to forestall any change to the habits of his family.

'In Portugal they eat at the table, Grandfather!' Chandracanta exclaimed with a slight air of superiority.

But the old man was having none of it. 'I've had it up to here with what they do in Portugal. Since your return, you've not talked about anything else.'

Sadassiva thought the argument pointless. Greatly perturbed, he decided to set his son straight immediately. He recalled being the only one who'd supported the idea of having a doctor in the family. But it wouldn't do to go to extremes. Wiping the sweat from his brow, he said: 'Your grandfather is right, Chandra! Since your return, all you've done is shove your new habits in our faces. Are you no longer the old Chand just because you've become a doctor?'

From the far end of the corridor, Dhruva was eavesdropping on the conversation but couldn't make out all the words. On the pretext of clearing the metal plates away she sidled in. She too felt that this Chandracanta was not the one she'd been given as a husband those six years ago; then, although a stranger, she hadn't needed words to understand him. Now he was more than a stranger—he was an outsider.

Seeing his daughter-in-law moving to clear away the plates, Sadassiva paused, accustomed to not discussing important matters before womenfolk. He felt impatient, as he hadn't managed to express all he'd wanted to say. It then occurred to him to go outside and smoke a bidi. Sadassiva was just about to ask for a light when he realized that his son was no longer there.

'Chandracanta, hey Chand!' he called out, ready to continue the conversation where they'd left off.

The grandfather gave a gesture of annoyance.

'Chand is the only one who wears his shoes indoors,' he grumbled cantankerously, pointing to the scuffmarks Chandracanta had left behind him on the floor.

Chandracanta had gone out. He needed to be alone, to find some inner peace. And he thought about himself, about those Goans who never returned home, and regretted not having done likewise, not having left with Luísa for Mozambique. The memory of Luísa brought to mind his time in Lisbon, the afternoons they'd spent together on the Avenida da Liberdade, in the Jardim Botânico . . . But now that had all gone, everything, it was too late, far too late. Now he was back home and had to start his life as a young physician in Pangim. The idea of spending his whole life there brought on a feeling of defeat and, as if his strength were giving out, he looked around for a place to sit. There was a large rock nearby. This time he didn't get his handkerchief out but sat down unflinchingly on the dirty stone.

He would have stayed there for a long time, engrossed in his own pessimism, if someone hadn't tapped him on the shoulder.

'What are you doing here, Chandracanta?' he heard a voice exclaim.

He turned to face the interloper.

The old man continued, a little abashed: 'Don't you recognize me? It's Caxinata Sirvodcar . . . '

'Oh, yes . . . yes, I didn't recognize you . . . that's to say . . . ' he stammered, frowning. 'You're . . . you were my Marathi teacher! So many years ago now . . . '

'But I haven't forgotten you. They tell me you've become a doctor. I'm most happy!' The teacher chuckled contentedly, displaying the few teeth that remained. 'And what do you make of all this, huh? Just the same old, same old, no?'

As if wanting to discard an old rag, Chandracanta remarked: 'I'm fed up with it! If I could, I'd take myself straight back to Portugal!'

Caxinata didn't hide the deep pain this remark caused him.

'When you youngsters go to Portugal you don't like it here any more! Or you pretend not to, to make yourselves out as big shots! If everybody thought like you and the others who leave never to return, then Goa would be abandoned to the infants and the elderly . . . ' He threw the butt of his finished cigarette to the ground and crushed it underfoot. His sombre expression was absorbed by the dark night quickly falling. 'You, the children of Goa . . . ' he continued passionately. But his voice failed him, as if faced with something irremediable: 'You refuse . . . you refuse . . . you refuse to make this place any better . . . ' And off he trudged, gesticulating to himself and abandoning Chandracanta to his perplexity.

As he watched the withered figure of his old teacher fade slowly into the gloom, Chandracanta caught sight of the time. It was nine o'clock. They'll all be asleep no doubt, he thought sadly.

With no destination in mind, he lumbered along in the direction taken by his old teacher, which was also his own way home. 'He must be right. His opinion is in harmony with the land, and the land is right, always,' he murmured. 'I'm the one who left and who didn't want to come home.' In the sky, like a streak of sparkles, he seemed to see the image of his grandfather. He shivered. He couldn't work out whether this was from the wind blowing out towards the sea or his regret for the way in which he had spoken to the old man. Chandracanta considered how his family had never left their land, where they lived just as they had for millennia, in accordance with the traditions of their caste. He now saw his mother as the cornerstone of their family. And Dhruva? What of Dhruva? He looked up into the darkened sky once more and, as always, saw a star shining bright, the pole star, Dhruva. Dhruva was now no longer a robot—she was as her name symbolized, the faithful, steadfast wife who had waited six years for his return. He wanted to dash to her but the path was narrow and he had to mind the snakes that, startled by his footsteps, might shoot forth enraged from their lairs.

Chandracanta placed his shoes next to the sandals of his father and his grandfather, as he had been taught as a boy, the tradition of many generations. In the heavy silence of the house, only a small light flickered. He followed it, timorous yet full of hope. It was a candle burning before the image of the goddess Lakshmi. He paused for a moment. Deep inside, everything had been laid to waste. He knew now that he had to depart once more—to return to the twentieth century, to today.

Glossary

aai: mother

abolim: small red flower of Goa

ailé-belé: sweet made of rice flour, jaggery and coconut

alalala: Interjection of appreciation; 'How beautiful!'

apai: grandfather

apas: Indo-Portuguese term for chapati

ay! Kata-kata: interjection of pity or sorrow

bab, baba: respectful and affectionate form of address for men or boys. Often post-fixed to their given names

baiee-faiee: gushing pleasantries

bai/baiee: respectful and affectionate forms of address for married women / unmarried women; often post-fixed to their given names

bhatcar, bhatcara: rural landowner, for whom mundcars work, derived from Konkani 'bhat' (land) and -car (a suffix indicating control); bhatcan, bhatcarina (fem.)

bodki: widow, forbidden to remarry

bom dia: good day (Port.)

Bonguis: lower-caste manual scavengers; Hindi: Bhangi

cadeira voltaire: voltaire chair (Port.). Named for the French Enlightenment writer, it is a wooden easy chair with long footrests, typical of comfortably-off Goan homes

cambolim: heavy woollen cape

canji: local variant of congee, a rice porridge or gruel boiled in and water

capodd: sari worn by married women

Chardó: the second Catholic caste, equivalent to Kshatriyas

chinchré: dry tamarind seeds

chondor-vatt: incense

churtas: palm leaf

confraria: literally 'brotherhood' or 'confraternity' (Port.). Refers to caste-specific associations within a parish

corangute: type of coarse-grain rice, normally cooked in the husk

Curumbim (pl. Curumbins): lower-caste agricultural labourers

dadda: father

descendentes: descendants of European families that lived in Goa for centuries. Often of mixed race, they always struggled to be recognized as European with its attendant benefits

deva: God

dhumti: variety of thick hand-rolled cigarette; Hindi: bidi

distican: woman faith healer, who is thought to be able to deflect the evil-eye.

divtti: small earthen lamp commonly found in Goan Hindu households; Hindi: diya

doulo (pl. doulé): spoon made from coconut shell

Faraz (pl. Farazes): lower-caste bamboo weavers

feni: alcohol distilled from cashew fruit or toddy palm, typical of Goa gaddi: witchdoctor

gasolina: small, simple river ferry (Port.)

goddé: marbles

hus!: hostile interjection

irani: eating-house, historically run by Zoroastrian Iranis

jagrada: sweet made from jaggery (from Portuguese 'jagra', meaning jaggery, and 'ada', a suffix indicating a quantity or product of something)

Jayadeva: twelfth-century Sanskrit poet

jhele: garlands of flowers for the hair

kaku: uncle

kum kum: pigment worn on the foreheads of Hindu women

langotim (pl. langotins): loincloth

lotação: omnibus as called in Brazil (Port.)

mai: mother in Konkani (from Portuguese 'mãe')

mano / mana: informal forms of brother / sister (Port.)

mundcar: tenant; derived from 'mund' (referring to a debt incurred for the construction of a dwelling on the bhatcar's land) and –car (a suffix here indicating association)

nachni: a variety of millet, often sown onto nativity scenes to provide grass

nattak (pl. nattakan): Indian popular theatre, traditionally performed near temples

oddé: Goan deep-fried sweets typically eaten at Christmas

olas: woven palm leaves

orchata: drink made from ground almonds and sugar (Port.)

paclo (pl. paclé): name given to the Portuguese (possibly from the Konkani 'pakh', meaning feather, in reference to the white plume once adorning Portuguese soldiers' caps) palov: tip of the sari, which is thrown back over the shoulders or used to cover the head

polkist: a polka-dancer, used in the text ironically to refer a dancer performing a comical jig

puddvem: dress cloth that Hindu males substitute for trousers

rasa: 'flavour', figurative emotion that the actor should communicate to the audience

saiba: vocative of Saib, lord

sapai: father-in-law

saudade: nostalgia, longing (Port.)

suné: daughter-in-law

tali: one of the ceremonies in Hindu weddings; a beaded, saffron coloured thread which goes around the bride's neck

tambio: metal jug for washing

tanga: small copper coin, equal in value to the Indian anna. In circulation until 1958, the Portuguese Indian Rupia was divided into sixteen tangas

tiatr: Christian popular theatre, similar to Portuguese revues, very popular in the villages of Goa, constituting an important vehicle for social criticism

tio / tia: aunt / uncle (Port.). A diminutive form is 'ti'; akin to aunty

tornaboda: final celebration held the day after a wedding at the home of the bride (Port.)

urrak: alcohol derived from the first distillation of feni

xacuti: spicy dish, usually containing lamb or kid goat

zaieu: white flower of Goa